**"You could," Trevor told
her definitely,
"seduce Mount Rushmore—
all four of them—
in that dress."**

"What works on granite doesn't work on man?" Taylor said wistfully.

"This man is putty in your hands," he assured her in a rueful voice. "You came loaded for bear and found a puppy instead."

She giggled. "Then I won't have to strip down to the teddy to get your attention?" she asked innocently.

To his throat-clearing, Trevor added swallowing. She'd caught him at a perfect time, while he was hovering between what he wanted and what he knew he couldn't have. He could have strangled her. Except that he wanted her in his arms worse than he'd ever wanted anything in his life . . .

Kay Robbins

Prolific author Kay Robbins hails from a western North Carolina town so tiny "it could fit in a single snapshot," within a community so close-knit "the mailman will come looking for me if he doesn't find me at home." Though Kay lives alone (except for her "arrogant" cat, Sonny) in a house she co-designed and her father built, life is seldom lonely. Her brother is her next-door neighbor, her parents live next door to him, and her sister lives next door to their parents!

A true animal lover, last year Kay acquired a quarter-horse mare—before she found out it was pregnant. Her friends often wonder just how large her menagerie will grow...

Thoroughly dedicated to her writing, Kay occasionally diverts herself with voracious reading, televised baseball, solitaire, and jigsaw puzzles. As Belonging to Taylor attests, she has a continuing fascination with psychic phenomena. She's also a fond collector of unicorns and dragons.

Dear Reader:

For all you Kay Robbins fans, here's a brand-new reason to cheer: *Belonging to Taylor* (#322). Beautiful psychic Taylor Shannon knows Trevor King is the man she's destined to marry. But, as any self-respecting male would, Trevor has his doubts about "belonging" to *anyone*. Told by the beleaguered hero as he manfully resists seduction, *Belonging to Taylor* offers all the wit and whimsy you've come to expect from Kay Robbins ... and a serious exploration of the wondrous meaning of true love. Humorous and dramatic, playful and poignant, *Belonging to Taylor* is a romance to cherish.

A high-tech genius may not be the usual stuff of which heroes are made, but in *Anywhere and Always* (#323) by Lee Williams, brilliant, offbeat Justin Fuller is a quintessential heartthrob. Arriving in Lydie Henley's hometown for an enforced vacation, Justin astounds her with inventive wizardry, catches her off-guard with amazing insights, and completely sweeps her away. How can she resist a man who so eagerly anticipates her lessons in "How to Relax Away From a Computer"? How can she say no to a disheveled sweetheart who's apt to forget to go to bed ... unless she's there to entice him? *Anywhere and Always* will leave you with a smile and a sigh.

In *Fortune's Choice* (#324), Elissa Curry pairs another of her "bad boy" heroes, handsome rogue Nick Parmenter, with slightly spoiled socialite "Joey" Fortune, whose father has finally tied the purse strings and thrust her out into the cold, cold world. What's more logical than for two such ne'er-do-wells to join forces in a risky venture—selling ice cream? Of course, they survive poverty in high style *and* contend with a slimy fortune-hunter, some wily gangsters, and a resourceful priest. Reading *Fortune's Choice* is like watching a 1930's romantic comedy. Hepburn and Tracy, move over!

I'm thrilled to introduce Cait Logan, a talented newcomer whose *Lady on the Line* (#325) may remind you of the work of another of our popular authors, Ann

Cristy. Like Ann, Cait Logan creates the larger-than-life heroes we all dream about—men who are masculine in *every* sense of the word. Barrett Redding makes K.C. Bollins feel *very* womanly, and he wants nothing more than to protect her. But K.C. is used to taking care of herself and her son, to surviving in a tough world. Yet she's scorched by the heat of Barrett's hungry gaze ... *Lady on the Line* is a real sizzler!

Seldom do women *like* turning forty, and the heroine of *A Kiss Away* (#326) by Sherryl Woods is no exception. Jessica Warren plans to greet the big "four-oh" with a dose of maturity *and* a physically fit body. But her new exercise plan sends her limping into the sympathetic—and irritatingly muscular—arms of her gorgeous neighbor, Kevin Lawrence. In no time Kevin's boyish energy, disregard for propriety, and shamelessly erotic pursuit have Jessica's hormones hopping. Sherryl Woods brings us both humor and a mature love story.

If you thrill to the stories of the silver screen, then *Play It Again, Sam* (#327) by Petra Diamond is the romance for you. To incurably nostalgic Nedda Shaw, Brooklyn-born costume designer Sam Harrison is about as foreign as they come. Sam brazenly vows to drag Nedda kicking into the twentieth century—and his bed—but he soon learns that the only way to a Southern belle's body is through her heart. As Sam gamely attempts an old-fashioned courtship, both he and Nedda are perplexed, and thrilled, to discover true love!

Until next month, warmest wishes,

Ellen Edwards

Ellen Edwards, Senior Editor
SECOND CHANCE AT LOVE
The Berkley Publishing Group
200 Madison Avenue
New York, NY 10016

SECOND CHANCE AT LOVE™

KAY ROBBINS
BELONGING TO TAYLOR

A
SECOND CHANCE AT LOVE
BOOK

For Eileen:
"This rough magic"

O! she's warm.
If this be magic, let it be an art
Lawful as eating.

—William Shakespeare,
The Winter's Tale

BELONGING TO TAYLOR

Chapter One

TREVOR KING HAD never thought of himself as a busy-body, but when a man came across a young lady crying her eyes out noisily in the middle of a very lovely and peaceful garden, he decided, there was surely some justification for trying to find out what was going on. Accordingly, he sat down on the stone bench beside the distressed damsel and asked a pointed question.

"Excuse me, but what in hell is wrong?"

Stunningly electric blue eyes, no less potent for being tear-drenched, gazed at his face for a moment and then were hidden once more behind slender fingers as the dam burst in earnest.

Conscious of innate male helplessness when confronted by irrational female tears, Trevor ran bewildered fingers through his thick black hair and stared at her warily. Those incredible eyes, he reflected in astonishment, had held a rueful gleam of amusement. Hysteria? he wondered, studying her long, lustrous chestnut hair—which was all he could really see.

No, not hysteria. He didn't know why he was so sure of that, but he was. Sighing, and wryly condemning his own curiosity, he dug in his pocket for a handkerchief and held it out to her. "Here," he offered brusquely.

She couldn't have seen it through her tears and fingers, but she reached out anyway to grasp the snowy cloth and press it to her eyes.

Trevor gazed off across the garden, waiting patiently for time or exhaustion to stem the tide. It took another five minutes before the sobs lessened to sniffles and finally faded into silence. He heard her blow her nose fiercely and turned his head to intercept another curiously amused look from those wet, vivid blue eyes.

"I—uh—I have this problem," she murmured.

"I guessed as much," he responded politely.

She squared her shoulders and met his bemused gaze defiantly. "I cry," she announced as though to a blind man with bad hearing. "I cry over sad movies, sad books, the national anthem, and commercials with cute kids and puppies. I cry over spring showers, rainbows, bad days, *good* days, and dead butterflies. I cry," she summed up, leaning forward to emphasize the point, "when my *laundry* comes back!"

Trevor blinked. He found himself gazing into a striking face, in which the electric blue eyes dominated all other features. He was vaguely conscious of a small nose, high cheekbones, straight winging brows, cupid-bow lips, and a stubborn chin. Viewed separately, the features didn't seem to fit together, and yet they made a more than pleasing whole. In fact, it was an endlessly fascinating face.

And there were absolutely no signs of the tears that had so recently halted. No red-rimmed eyes. No pink nose. No flushed splotches.

Resolutely, Trevor pulled himself together. "What were you crying about this time?" he asked.

"Oh, don't! You'll start me off again!" She caught her underlip firmly between white teeth to stop a slight quiver, then apparently controlled a last urge to sob again. "It wasn't important anyway. It never is," she added in the wry tone of someone resigned to a troublesome but irrepressible trait.

Trevor grappled with that for a moment in silence. "I see. Then you're all right?"

"Oh, yes. It was kind of you to be concerned, though."

Given an opportunity to accept her thanks and walk away, he found himself unable to do any such thing. "My name's Trevor King," he said as if it was an afterthought.

She gravely held out the hand not clutching the handkerchief. "I'm Taylor Shannon."

As his fingers closed around her slender ones, Trevor felt a very curious sensation. Startled, he stared down at their hands, aware of what felt like a genuine electric shock and then a spreading warmth. A soothing blanket crept up his arm, over his shoulder, and down his body, lending a feeling of security that was as strong as it was surprising.

"Well!" She, too, was staring at their clasped hands. Then her vivid eyes lifted to his face, and there was something in them he almost flinched from because it was so nakedly honest. "I'll be damned," she added blankly.

He rather hastily reclaimed his hand, feeling it tingle as it left hers. And the "security blanket" left him as if it had been a visible quilt ripped away.

"I didn't expect to meet you so soon," she said thoughtfully.

"What?" he managed, but she was going on, unhearing.

"It's really not the best time. In another five years, I would have— Oh, well. It's no use fighting these things. But I don't know anything about you," she accused irritably, staring at him. "You might be an ax murderer or something!"

"I'm not," he offered somewhat weakly, unable to get even the slightest handle on what was going on.

She was abruptly cheerful. "Oh, I know that! You like kids and animals; your favorite color is blue; you love Italian food and old movies; you live alone—at the moment," she added sapiently. "You have a younger brother who adores you, and you're a criminal lawyer."

Trevor was unable to hide his astonishment. "How'd you know all that?" he demanded.

She cocked an eyebrow at him. "On target?"

"All the way across the board!"

"That clinches it," she said cryptically. "I've never

gotten so much from one touch."

He flexed the fingers that had held her hand, looking down at them for a moment. Then he stared at her warily. "Who are you?"

"Don't you mean what am I?" she corrected, seemingly amused.

"All right, then—*what* are you?"

"I'm the woman you're going to marry," she told him solemnly.

"I beg your pardon?"

Taylor began laughing. "Don't look so horrified! It'll probably work out very well, you know. You have more than a spark yourself, and that'll make things even better."

"A spark of what?" he asked, choosing the lesser of two evils.

"Raw talent."

Trevor ran fingers through his hair and stared at her. He couldn't help wondering if this undeniably fascinating woman was spending the odd day away from the funny farm, but he couldn't seem to make himself get up and walk away from her. "I don't know what we're talking about," he confessed finally.

She laughed again. "I'm sorry—I seem to have overpowered you! It's a fault of mine, I'm afraid, because I've lived with psychics so long I sometimes forget others aren't so familiar with it. We're talking about 'esper'—that's shorthand for psychic or parapsychological—abilities; that's what you have a spark of raw talent in."

He shook his head instantly. "I don't believe in that stuff."

Taylor sighed. "Oh, dear. I can just see the rocks looming in my path. If you don't believe, I've got my work cut out for me."

Ignoring this, he said firmly, "Jason put you up to this; that's how you knew so much about me."

"I've never met your brother."

"Then how d'you know Jason's my brother?" he pounced.

"The same way I know so much about you." She sighed again, murmuring to herself, "Parlor tricks. I knew it'd come to parlor tricks. And I hate them. Why did fate do this to me?"

"If you can read my mind—" he began, challenging.

"I'm way ahead of you," she interrupted dryly. "You want proof. You want me to do something that will instantly convince you I'm psychic. All right then, dammit—if it's parlor tricks you want, parlor tricks you shall have! Think of something very obscure—something only you know. Something I couldn't *possibly* have learned from anyone else."

She held out her hand commandingly, and Trevor, with only an instant's hesitation, closed his fingers around hers. He felt the warm blanket creeping up his shoulder, closed his mind to that, and began to concentrate.

Taylor's face was serene, her vivid eyes fixed on his face. And when she spoke, it was not in some blurred, trancelike voice, but in a calm and matter-of-fact tone.

"You're very young. There's a man you know. A friend of your parents. No, more than that. He's your godfather. He did something—no. They *said* he did something. They said he killed a man. You know he couldn't have done it. You think his lawyer believes him guilty. You think that's why he's been convicted. And why he's—"

She broke off abruptly as Trevor jerked his hand away. Apparently undisturbed by his sudden retreat, she gazed into his shocked eyes and said quietly, "I see. That's why you decided to become a lawyer. And you never told anyone that, did you." It wasn't a question.

Trevor drew a deep, shaken breath. "My God," he said unsteadily.

After looking at him for a moment, she began to talk lightly. "I'm like a sponge—soaking up information. It doesn't tire me, which is a bit uncommon among psychics. It *does* tire me if I have to reach out farther than touch; for instance, if I'm trying to find someone and have only a bit of clothing or jewelry to go on. My mother's a touch-telepath, too. Daddy's the precognitive one; I inherited a bit of his talent, but I'm not too strong in that, thank God."

Stirring slightly, Trevor made an attempt to untangle the threads of disbelief, panic, and finally belief. He only partially succeeded, but he was grateful for her obvious intention to give him time to get hold of himself. "Why . . . thank God?" he murmured.

"About not being strongly precognitive?" She shook her head slightly. "Looking into the future isn't usually comfortable. You tend to see disasters rather than triumphs. Thankfully, Daddy can't see his own future or that of anyone he really cares about. And I just see bits and pieces."

Recalling the troubling statement she'd made,

Trevor challenged, "Then how d'you know we'll be married?"

"Oh, that's different," she told him cheerfully. "I knew that instantly, the moment I touched you. I always expected to know, but I really didn't think it'd be this soon."

"How old are you?" he demanded suddenly.

"Twenty-six. And you're thirty-two, right?"

"Right," he sighed, wondering if 'esper' abilities became more believable simply by being casually discussed. He found his own disbelief fading—speeded along by her earlier demonstration—and a growing discomfort taking its place.

She was smiling just a little. "That's always the second reaction," she mused softly. "First comes disbelief—then comes discomfort. Then fear."

He looked at her for a moment, seeing no self-pity in her remarkable eyes, but aware, suddenly, that it couldn't be a good feeling to inspire fear in others. Instinctively trying to close down his own mind—and uneasily aware that fear drove him—he changed the subject. "Surely you weren't serious about marriage?"

Taylor seemed disturbed for the first time. She looked at him, the naked honesty in her eyes, her face hurt. "Is the idea so distasteful to you?" she asked diffidently.

Gazing at that fascinating, hurt face, Trevor was disarmed totally against his will. "It isn't that," he said with more firmness than he'd intended. "But we're strangers! I mean—well, *I* can't pick facts about you out of thin air. Besides, I don't like having my future planned for me. And, if you want brutal honesty, I don't much like the idea of having a wife who reads minds!"

Oddly, she seemed less disturbed now. "Well, if that's all it is," she said dismissively. "I was afraid the thought of seeing my face across the breakfast table was giving you the horrors."

He laughed in spite of himself. "Hardly that. You . . . have a fascinating face, Taylor Shannon. I suspect there's a lot about you I'd find fascinating. However," he added hastily, "the timing isn't right for me either. I'm at the midway point of a vacation, after which I have a heavy load of court cases." He got to his feet.

What was intended to be a polite and final leave-taking turned out to be no such thing. Taylor rose to her feet also, looking up at him hopefully. "I don't want to impose," she said guilelessly, "but could you possibly give me a ride home? It's getting dark, and—"

"Of course." Uneasily suspicious, Trevor was nonetheless too polite to question her motives. He glanced down as she walked beside him along the path, noting absently that the top of her head barely reached his heart.

It was difficult to see clearly now in the gathering twilight, but he'd already noticed that her blue jogging suit and shoes closely matched his own red outfit. It was casual, comfortable wear, seen often on the streets these days and not always meant as exercise suits. He'd not been jogging himself, but rather had driven out here for what he'd meant to be a half hour or so of air and scenery.

And found a crying psychic! he chided himself mentally.

Taylor seemed content to walk in silence, saying

nothing until they reached his car. Then she looked at the hulking Jeep and laughed delightedly. "I knew it! Rugged, strong, and practical—just like you!"

Not entirely sure he liked the comparison, Trevor merely opened the passenger door and gestured silently. When he went around to his own side and climbed in, he found Taylor staring intently at the stuffed unicorn hanging from the rearview mirror. She sent him a glance as he started the engine, and he wasn't quite certain he had caught her words.

He hoped he hadn't, hoped that with the intensity of a man caught in some act believed to be unmanly. Had she really said something about the soul of a dreamer?

The Jeep, in accordance with Taylor's directions, drew into the driveway of a large three-story house possessing that indefinable air of having been lived in over many years. Trevor felt curiously drawn to the house; it was a sensation he'd never felt before and now profoundly distrusted.

Deciding that this leave-taking *would* be final, he opened his mouth to utter some polite and evasive words.

But he never got the chance.

The side door of the house, located by the drive, burst open just then, revealing a girl who looked nothing at all like Taylor. She was raven-haired, tomboyish, definitely tousled, and all of ten years old. Literally swarming up Taylor's side of the Jeep, she peered through the open window and shrieked, "Taylor! Agamemnon stole Mother's best blouse and Dad says the preacher's coming and Solomon's had her kittens *somewhere* and Jamie lost my *favorite* sheets and Dory's locked herself in the closet *again* and won't come out and somebody let Jack and Jill loose and I think they're under the washing machine and Solomon will *eat* them unless I get them out and we've got *chicken* for supper and *please* can't you *do* something or I'm going to join a *nunnery!*"

And, putting a period to her extraordinary sentence, the moppet slid back down the side of the Jeep and vanished into the house.

Murmuring, "Oh, dear," Taylor opened her door. Glancing back over her shoulder at her stunned companion, she added cheerfully, "Come on in."

And Trevor, betrayed once more by his curiosity, followed her meekly into the house.

Chapter Two

TREVOR HAD LITTLE opportunity to note the furnishings of the house, for the inmates instantly overpowered everything else. He found himself standing in a den and had the general impression of tasteful decorating overlaid by the clutter of a lively and populous family. There were various clashes, bangs, and thumps coming from distant parts of the house; in this room, the moppet's strident voice reigned.

Taylor was ignoring the importunities of her sister in order to ask a brief question of a strikingly lovely raven-haired woman.

"Which, Mother?"

Standing in the center of the room, Mrs. Shannon, who was dressed in jeans and a peasant blouse but

13

wore vagueness like a cloud, blinked gray eyes at her daughter. "The blouse, I think, darling," she said in a soft lilting voice. "Because of the Reverend. Then Dory out of the closet; she wanted you and you weren't here, so she hid. Your father's looking for the kittens."

"My sheets!" the moppet wailed, tugging at Taylor's sleeve.

Taylor removed the fierce clasp on her sleeve, saying briskly, "Help me find the blouse, Jessie; then we'll find your sheets." She led the protesting child from the room.

Trevor found himself the focus of vague gray eyes. "Hello," she said encouragingly. "Any good with hamsters?"

He blinked, not really sure what was expected of him. "Animals in general," he offered.

A slight frown disturbed her beautiful face, then vanished. "It'll have to do," she said in the tone of one who didn't expect a miracle. "Jamie—the hamsters."

From an adjoining room came a slender wraith of a girl. About sixteen or so, she was blond and bore the same mismatched, fascinating features of her sisters eclipsed by the dreamy gray eyes of her mother.

"All right, Mother," she said softly. She took Trevor's hand and led him, unresisting, down a short hallway and into a laundry room. Then she sat on a tall stool and gestured toward the washing machine. "They're under there, we think," she said helpfully.

Presented with a definite task—however bizarre— Trevor felt some relief. He pushed up his sleeves, stretched out on the floor, and worked one arm around behind the machine.

"It'd be easier," he panted, feeling around gingerly, "to pull the washer away from the wall. But there's no room."

"And it's bolted to the floor," Jamie explained serenely. "It walked around and made noise, so Daddy fixed it. Do you belong to Taylor?" she added politely.

Disconcerted, Trevor peered up at her even as he found and grasped a warm, furry body in his searching hand. Suppressing a wild impulse to answer, "I think so," he pulled the hamster from under the machine and said instead, "Want to hold this while I get the other one?"

Jamie bent forward to accept the hamster, cuddling it against her sweater. "Nobody but Daddy has an arm long enough," she said suddenly. "And he's looking for the kittens."

Again disconcerted, Trevor realized that she'd answered his mental question: why no one had retrieved the hamsters before now. Remembering something Taylor had said earlier, he thought, *Oh, Lord—all of them?*

He found the second hamster and held it in one hand as he got to his feet. "Where do they belong?" he asked, perforce adopting the verbal shorthand of the family.

"They live in Dory's room. I'll take them up." She got the second hamster and stepped toward the door, pausing only to smile at him over her shoulder. "I hope you belong to Taylor. I like you," she said naively.

Trevor stood there for a moment, absently pulling his sleeves down, then sighed and made his way back to the den. He wondered in sudden amusement when it would occur to this absurd family that there was a total stranger in their midst; he had a feeling it might never happen.

Reaching the den, he found Taylor's mother exactly as he'd left her. She stared into the middle distance but turned her head when he came into the room. "Name?" she asked abruptly.

"Trevor," he answered a bit helplessly.

She appeared to consider. "Good. That's good. Two syllables and the same first and last letters. Last name?"

"King," he supplied.

After a brief frown, she nodded, satisfied. "Not bad. At least, unless there's a German shepherd in the room."

"I beg your pardon?" he managed, faint but pursuing.

"They always name them Prince or King," she explained vaguely. "Confusing if you're in the same room."

Trevor leaned against a wall for support, staring in utter fascination at the woman. He couldn't, for the life of him, get a handle on Taylor's mother. The niggling suspicion that she was hardly as vague as she seemed wasn't confirmed by any outward sign, but his courtroom-sharpened senses told him there was much more to the lady.

Before anything else could be said, Taylor returned to the den. Under one arm she carried a clearly disgusted toy poodle, and in her free hand was the missing blouse. Jessie skipped impatiently at her side, still nattering about her mislaid sheets, and a newcomer clung fiercely to the jacket of Taylor's warm-up suit.

The newcomer, Trevor decided, must be Dory. If Jessie was a talkative moppet and Jamie a serene wraith, then Dory was a pixie. She was all of six years old, her red hair cut short around a face uncannily like her sisters'. But in her small face glowed the huge, vivid blue eyes only Taylor shared.

That there was an affinity between the two was obvious; Dory stared up at her sister adoringly, and Taylor, after handing the blouse to her mother, reached to absently smooth shaggy red hair.

Trevor was trying to convince himself silently that he really should leave when he realized he was under scrutiny. Dory had released her grip on her sister and crossed to stand before him, looking up at him solemnly.

Instinctively going down on one knee to be closer to eye level with the child, he returned her stare as gravely as she offered it. "Hello," he said gently.

"Hello." Not a piping, childish voice, but one far too gruff and serious for the young face. And, astonishing the man, she asked the same question her sister had asked. "D'you belong to Taylor?"

He found himself uncomfortable beneath that solemn stare as he'd not been with Jamie; this one, he knew, wouldn't accept evasion. "I just met her," he explained seriously.

She frowned a little as if the answer was unsatisfying, then reached out and laid a tiny hand on his shoulder. A shy, elusive smile flitted briefly across her mismatched features and was gone. But she nodded to herself as she withdrew her hand. "You belong to Taylor," she told him firmly, her tone that of a wise teacher for a dim pupil.

Trevor blinked. She wandered away before he could say anything, and he rose to his feet slowly. He saw that Mrs. Shannon had vanished—apparently to don the found blouse—and watched as Dory stood on tiptoe to whisper into Taylor's attentive ear before wandering from the room.

"My sheets!" Jessie cried impatiently. "Taylor!"

"All right, Jess!" Taylor glanced around briefly, then said dryly, "They're in the piano bench, where you left them! Next time, don't blame your absent-mindedness on Jamie."

Taylor turned to Trevor as her sister shot from the room, exclaiming immediately, "Hasn't anyone asked you to sit down? Do, for heaven's sake!"

He removed a Teddy bear from a chair and sat down, telling himself that he merely needed to recruit his strength before fleeing the madhouse. "D'you have a mirror?" he asked carefully.

She sank down in a chair across from his, still holding the poodle and gazing at him quizzically. "Not on me. Why?"

"Because I think there's a brand of possession on my forehead, and I'd like to see it."

Taylor laughed. "Have they been pestering you? I'm sorry!"

He sighed. "Not pestering. Just asking in the most natural, innocent way if I belong to you."

"And what did you answer?"

"I evaded Jamie's question. I told Dory—I assume the little one's Dory—that I'd just met you. That didn't satisfy her; she touched my shoulder and then told me reprovingly that I belonged to you." He reflected for a moment, adding thoughtfully, "And your mother liked the sound of my name but hopes there won't be a German shepherd in the room, since they're always named Prince or King."

Taylor was giggling. "My family's a little . . . original," she gasped. "I should have warned you."

"Are *all* of you psychic?" he demanded.

She nodded. "To varying degrees. Of my sisters, Jessie has the least natural ability and Dory the most. And Jamie's sporadic; we never know whether she'll predict tomorrow's news or ask someone to help her find a lost shoe."

Before Trevor could respond, a tall, disheveled blond man appeared in the doorway leading to the main hall, announcing in a deep, satisfied tone, "I've found the kittens."

He earned Taylor's instant attention. "Oh, good! Where?"

"In that old sewing basket some idiot got your mother years ago," her father explained. "There's never been any sewing in it, so it's perfect."

Trevor, on his feet and watching silently, noted that Taylor and Dory had gotten their electric blue eyes from their father. He also noticed that both parents looked ridiculously young. At a guess, they were both in their fifties, but neither looked a day over thirty-five. *Does being psychic make you age slower?* he wondered abstractedly, then realized that a vivid but benign stare had fixed on him.

Then Taylor's father looked back at her. "Polite," he noted approvingly.

"Very," she agreed.

Her father bent a sudden frown on her. "No organ music, or I won't come! Your sister can play the piano, but I can't stand organs." He reflected for a moment, adding in the tone of a man who wishes to be clear, "Five kittens." Then he disappeared into the hall.

Trevor sank back into his chair.

After a single glance at his face, Taylor burst out laughing. "We're not crazy, I promise you! It's just that we forget how to talk to people outside the family, and when you get into the habit of not finishing sentences or even thoughts, it's very hard to remember."

"Try," he begged ruefully. "And would you mind explaining exactly what your father said? I think I missed most of it."

She smiled a little. "He said he found five kittens in an old sewing basket he got Mother years ago."

Trevor remembered the mildly uttered "some idiot" and wondered if Taylor's father often called himself that. "Yes, I got most of that, but what else did he say? Did he mean I was polite? And what was that about organs?"

"He meant you were polite—because you stood up when he came in. And that about organs was . . . um . . . in reference to weddings."

"One wedding in particular?" Trevor managed evenly.

"Uh-huh."

He stared at her. "Is there a shotgun pointed at me where I can't see it?" he asked finally.

"Of course not." Her smile was trying hard to hide.

"Then why does everyone in this house assume—

without even knowing my *name* for godsake—that I belong to you and that we're going to be married?"

Remaining silent, Taylor meditatively pulled at the poodle's ears and watched Trevor, clearly waiting for him to realize. He'd already realized, but he wasn't a man to go down without a fight.

"Because they're psychic?" he muttered.

She nodded.

Trevor made a valiant effort and produced a lightly mocking tone. "It's completely ridiculous. You realize that, don't you?"

"Completely," she agreed blandly.

"I mean, there is such a thing as free will."

"Certainly."

"I'm the captain of my fate," he insisted firmly. "The master of my soul. In charge of my own destiny."

Taylor nodded with grave agreement.

Glaring at her, Trevor said, "You don't believe a word I've said!"

"Of course I believe."

"But you also believe we'll get married?"

"I know we will."

Trevor dropped his head into his hands, massaging aching temples. "A prudent man," he said helplessly, "would run screaming into the night."

"Are you a prudent man?" she asked interestedly.

Lifting his head and gazing into those electric blue eyes, Trevor found to his disgust that he couldn't lay claim to prudence, logic, rationality, an instinct for self-preservation, or any other sane trait. "I think I've been bewitched," he groaned in answer.

She laughed, then asked briskly, "Can you cook?"

The very normality of the question was a welcome relief. "Yes."

"Good." She set the poodle on the floor and rose to her feet. "Mother's got the chicken baking, but I know she hasn't done anything else. Come help me."

Some moments later, Trevor found himself meekly donning a large chef's apron with HIS emblazoned across it in huge letters, while Taylor absently put on a matching one marked HERS. The kitchen was large and done in red brick and butcher-block counters, with copper pots hanging abundantly around a central work island. Everything was neat and clean, well-organized and arranged. And Trevor's instant feeling that this was Taylor's domain rather than her mother's was borne out by her cheerful words.

"I had the chicken ready to bake before I left this afternoon, and the oven all set. Mother's a disaster in the kitchen unless she has step-by-step instructions, and even then she's apt to wander off and forget she's left something on a burner."

Her tolerant amusement sparked Trevor's curiosity. He stepped around the poodle sniffing suspiciously at his trouser leg to obey her gesture and begin to prepare the ingredients she'd assembled for a salad. "Your mother can't be as vague as she looks," he objected, having finally realized that what may have seemed rude anywhere else was commonplace with this family.

Taylor laughed. "Well, she isn't, really. I mean, she's hopeless at most practical things. Cooking, cleaning, balancing a checkbook. If she goes to the store for a gallon of milk, she's likely to bring back shoes for Dory or a new collar for Agamemnon. Once she came home with a new car—and she got it for a really good price, too. We never did figure out how, because she doesn't seem to know how to bargain."

"But she isn't really vague?" Trevor prompted, amused.

"Not when it matters. She's got a disconcerting ability to go straight to the heart of things, and in a real emergency she's so efficient that it's scary." Pausing after whisking a cloth off homemade bread dough left to rise, Taylor looked reflective. "Daddy says he's terrified of her. He says she's the most utterly ruthless woman he's ever met in his life."

Trevor blinked, chopped cucumber for a moment, then said, "I have to hear about your father."

"Daddy?" She placed the loaf pan in the second of the two ovens, then straightened, thoughtful again. "Well, unlike Mother, who only says what she thinks is necessary, Daddy talks quite a lot. And you have to sift the chaff from the grain, if you know what I mean. He's apt to bury a vitally important sentence underneath a ton of absurdity. Animals adore him; I've seen totally wild creatures come up to him as gentle as you please and follow him around like puppies."

Scrabbling through a drawer, she located a ribbon, which she used to tie her long chestnut hair at the nape of her neck. Then she continued describing her father. "He cooks like a dream, can fix anything with an engine, and can do things with wood that'd have master cabinetmakers green with envy. He has a black belt in karate and was on the Olympic boxing team.

Oh—he's a doctor," she finished in an obvious afterthought.

"A medical doctor?" Trevor asked, surprised.

"Uh-huh."

"Chicken, Taylor!" wailed a voice suddenly from the doorway.

Taylor turned and stared, exasperated, at her sister. "Jessie, nobody's going to make you eat the chicken; there'll be bread and salad."

The moppet sighed and, slouching against the doorjamb, subjected Trevor to a long, thoughtful stare, as if she'd just noticed him. She, too, had gray eyes, he realized. And he could have predicted her sudden question.

"D'you belong to Taylor?"

Sighing, he threw Taylor a *See?* look and refused to answer.

"He's Trevor King," the oldest sister explained calmly. "Now, be helpful, Jessie, and go set the table."

Ignoring, for a moment, the request, Jessie straightened and said gloomily, "The preacher came, but just to drop off a flier about something. Mother's upstairs threatening to kill Daddy."

"Go set the table," Taylor repeated, and Jessie, with a last depressed sigh, vanished.

"Not seriously?" Trevor wondered aloud, not surprised when he didn't have to elaborate.

"Of course not. If I know Mother, she just said 'Dammit' and went off to change again. Jessie exaggerates. Constantly."

Trevor finally mentioned something that had been

hovering like a troublesome insect. "The blouse. A special blouse?"

"For the Reverend. And don't ask me why. Mother always wears that blouse when the Reverend comes." She giggled suddenly. "If he were a noticing kind of man, he'd probably wonder about that."

"But he isn't, darling."

The soft voice, wafting toward them from the doorway, startled Trevor. Taylor, of course, was undisturbed. "I suppose not, Mother."

Mrs. Shannon glided into the room with a feline grace that disconcerted Trevor; he realized only then that it was the first time he'd really seen her move. She was back in her jeans and peasant blouse, her raven hair caught at the nape of her neck like Taylor's. And she smiled vaguely on them both.

"Milk for Solomon, darling. Your father says."

Taylor nodded and went toward the refrigerator, snaring a bowl from a cabinet along the way.

Her mother continued to smile at Trevor. "I'm Sara. And Taylor's father is Luke. We forgot to tell you."

Rudderless yet again in her confusing wake, Trevor said uncertainly, "Nice to meet you . . . Sara."

She laughed softly, the gray eyes for a moment— an instant—not the slightest bit vague. There was something of the electric intensity of Taylor's eyes in them. Nothing at all threatening or ruthless, but an enormous strength and intelligence—and kindness. Then she was accepting the bowl from Taylor, and her eyes were vague again.

"Thank you, darling. Did I do it right?" she asked absently.

"Exactly right, Mother. Dinner in half an hour."

Sara Shannon drifted from the room, bearing the bowl of milk in both hands.

Trevor took a deep breath. "I agree with your father. She's frightening."

Giggling, Taylor said, "She must have turned the Power on you. Daddy says her eyes could topple mountains or stop armies in their tracks, but only when she *really* looks at something or someone. Strong men have been known to blench."

"Then," Trevor said definitely, "that's the way she just looked at me. I felt as if my dentist had just said all my teeth had to go."

Taylor laughed even harder. "I'll tell Mother that; she'll love it!"

He found himself staring intently at the clean, delicate line of her throat, his eyes skimming down over the small, slender body and back up to her fascinating face. And he thought *Hell, I am bewitched!* But that realization didn't lessen his sudden desire to kiss her.

"Trevor? Is something the matter?"

Abruptly, he demanded, "Can you always read thoughts when you touch someone? Always?"

"Oh, no," she denied instantly. "Some people instinctively mind-block. And the mood is an influence, too. It's funny, but strong emotions either broadcast powerfully or else throw up their own barriers."

In the grip of several strong emotions, Trevor decided to test the premise. At least, that's how he defended his actions to a sneering inner voice. He carefully laid aside the knife he was holding, wiped his hands thoroughly on a towel, and turned to Taylor.

Without giving her a chance to do or say anything, he drew her firmly into his arms and bent his head to hers.

He didn't really know what he was expecting, but he very quickly abandoned any pretense of "experimenting." And some dim and distant part of his mind wondered vaguely if "belonging to Taylor" meant having some indisputable right to these incredible feelings.

He'd felt desire before. And strong passion. What he'd never felt before was this odd, soul-deep warmth. He wanted to luxuriate in it, to bask in a golden glow of brilliant light and ... magic. Never before had he felt so completely, acutely aware of his own body as it literally *became* two bodies. He didn't believe what he felt, tried to disbelieve, but the essential *rightness* was too powerful to deny.

He knew the instant she took fire in his arms, felt the shiver of her body as if it were his own. He felt her little hands tangle in his hair, felt her rise on tiptoe to fit herself against him. Urgency gripped him; compulsion drove relentlessly toward an imperative, critically necessary joining.

But it was he who drew away suddenly, shaken by a violence of emotion that tore at something vital. *Just a kiss,* he thought dazedly, staring into vivid blue eyes that looked as shocked as he felt.

Taylor took a deep, unsteady breath and stepped back, automatically reaching to turn off the oven timer as it prosaically announced normality in a loud buzz. She turned off the oven itself with the same absentminded awareness, her eyes still fixed on Trevor. And when she spoke, she sounded as shaken as she looked.

"I've never felt anything like that before," she said, nakedly honest.

"Neither have I," he muttered hoarsely.

Taylor was quiet for a moment, gazing at him. Then she said with a sudden dry humor, "You really do think you're bewitched."

"Can you blame me?" he shot back. "All afternoon I've been told I'm going to marry you, asked if I belong to you, *told* I belong to you . . . And now this— this—"

"Feeling," she supplied quietly.

It stopped him cold. Shaking his head slightly, he said, "This is out of my league. I'd better go." He began fumbling with the ties of the apron, but she stopped him.

"No. You helped fix dinner; you'll stay for the meal at least. Besides, if you go now, Dory'll hide in the closet again."

He knew he was being betrayed again by curiosity, but he couldn't seem to help himself. "Why would she do that?" he asked blankly.

Taylor, completely herself again, was busily removing the chicken from one oven and the bread from another. Over her shoulder, she explained. "I told you that Dory has strong natural ability; she's very sensitive. And she hasn't learned to deal with herself yet, so practically anything sends her to hide in the closet. She likes you; if you leave so suddenly, it'll scare her."

A little diffidently, Trevor suggested, "Maybe she should be taken to see a . . . doctor."

"You mean a psychiatrist?" Taylor wasn't the least bit offended; she appeared to consider the suggestion seriously. "No, I don't think so. We all went through the same thing at her age: Jamie clung to Daddy, Jessie hid under her bed, and I was always creeping out into the woods by myself. We're all here for her when she needs us; that means a lot. She'll be fine."

"Dinner, Taylor?" asked a plaintive voice from the doorway. "Solomon's hidden the kittens again and Dory's lost Jack and I'm hungry."

"Just coming, Daddy," Taylor replied absently, concentrating on transferring the chicken from baking pan to serving dish.

"Your mother didn't ruin it?" her father asked anxiously.

"No, it's fine. Round everybody up, will you, please?"

"Yes, they're all waiting. But Jack? I suppose Trevor can get him out later if Solomon stays with her kittens and doesn't eat him. D'you play poker?" Luke Shannon demanded suddenly of Trevor.

"Yes." Trevor, an afternoon's accumulation of shocks and absurdities belatedly catching up with him, was holding on to control by force.

"Well, there's nothing to laugh about in that," Taylor's father chided reprovingly, shattering the last remnants of Trevor's control. Gazing at his daughter's guest as he leaned against the refrigerator and laughed himself silly, Luke directed an interested question to his daughter. "Is he staying, Taylor?"

"For dinner, at least," she murmured, crossing to hand her father the serving dish. "Take this in, Daddy."

"All right. Milk for your mother because of the baby, but I want wine."

Taylor nodded and turned back to quickly and efficiently slice the bread, watching with amusement as Trevor's laughter was cut short and replaced by astonishment.

"Your mother's—?"

"Pregnant? Yes."

"But . . ." He didn't quite know how to frame his question.

Taylor laughed, understanding. "Her age? Mother's only forty-four, Trevor. I was born when she was eighteen. There's a certain risk for her age group, but her history is a good one. Our people tend to have large families and to space them all through the childbearing years. Mother says she was born to have babies because it's the only thing she does really well. But she also says this one's change-of-life and the last."

Removing his apron as she removed hers and automatically helping her gather the rest of the meal for transference to the dining room, Trevor reflected silently for a long moment. Then he began to laugh—silently this time.

"I wasn't ready for this," he muttered despairingly as he followed Taylor from the kitchen. "Nothing in life *prepared* me for this!"

Chapter Three

LOOKING BACK ON that meal later, Trevor realized that the hunted feeling he'd been conscious of had been more the result of his own acceptance of the situation than anything Taylor or her family said or did. It bothered him that he felt so comfortable so quickly, no longer startled or amazed, but simply quietly fascinated. The entire family had instantly and in their respectively vague, cheerful, solemn, offhand, or matter-of-fact ways accepted him as a part of them. And he began to enjoy it.

That was why he felt hunted. Absorption into this absurd family, however painless the process, boded ill for his bachelorhood. Not that he'd been clinging to *that* with rabid intensity, but a man liked to have

31

at least *some* say in the selection of his wife, he thought uneasily.

But when Dory, who had taken a chair beside his, slipped her tiny hand confidingly into his, and when he looked across the table to meet Taylor's smiling, vivid blue eyes, he found himself oddly disinclined to fight for his freedom.

Definitely hunted.

Taylor was aware, more by his reactions than anything else, that Trevor was still a bit unnerved. She watched his lean, handsome face across the dinner table, seeing the fascination, seeing his features soften whenever he looked at Dory, who sat so quietly beside him.

She watched him gradually relax in the company of her family, bemusement reflected in his keen gray eyes. He responded easily to any question or comment addressed to him, catching on quickly to the family's unconscious shorthand and even replying in kind after a fashion. Several times he seemed to swallow a sudden laugh, amusement lightening his rather stern eyes and curving the firm lips.

Lips.

Taylor ruthlessly dragged her mind away from memory and back to inspection. She was gazing at the man she would marry, and she knew that with a certainty that wouldn't be denied. She even could have told him how many children they'd have.

Psychic abilities, she thought ruefully—not for the first time—certainly took away some of life's little mysteries. Still, she didn't doubt that her trip to the altar would be troubled; Trevor, though accepting the clear proof of her abilities, was uncomfortable with them.

And they'd only known each other a matter of hours, after all.

Trevor found his apartment door unlocked and remembered even as he opened it that Jason had said something about stopping by. He found his brother stretched out on the couch, a bowl of popcorn on his flat stomach and a mug of beer in his hand as he stared at the television.

"Make yourself at home," Trevor invited dryly, tossing his keys onto a table in the foyer before stepping down into the living room.

"Don't mind if I do," Jason responded cheerily. He sat up and placed the bowl on the coffee table, smiling. Then his smile faded, and he came abruptly to his feet, staring at his brother. "What is it?" he asked in an altered voice.

"What?" Trevor responded blankly.

"You look like you've been hit by a train—mentally, that is."

Trevor sank down in a chair and frowned at his brother, irritated to hear that his tangled emotions showed so clearly on his face. "Well, I haven't," he said, further irritated by the defiance in his own voice.

Jason's eyebrows lifted and a grin began working at his mouth as he slowly sat back down. "Dare I guess the train was female?" he ventured solemnly.

"I wouldn't if I were you," Trevor warned.

Grinning openly now, Jason instantly demanded, "Who is she?"

"She isn't what you think!" Sighing, Trevor knew that Jason wouldn't give up until he heard at least part of the story. So he set his mind to editing certain things, telling the rest as briefly as possible.

"A whole family of psychics?" his brother exclaimed when he'd finished. "No wonder you look stunned. But I want to hear more about Taylor."

Trevor started slightly. He'd deliberately glossed over any details regarding Taylor, and his brother's ability to home in on that surprised him. After an evening with psychics, he hardly needed his own brother reading his mind. He sent Jason a guarded look; his brother was gazing back with innocently lifted brows. "Never mind Taylor."

"Why?"

"Because."

Jason chuckled. "So she's the one. I thought so, considering the way you carefully didn't mention her much."

Stirring restlessly, Trevor glared at the face that was a slightly younger edition of his own. "There's no 'one' and nothing to talk about," he said with great firmness.

Jason made a rude noise.

"Little brother, you've enjoyed my television set, my couch, my popcorn, and my beer—don't push your luck!"

His "little" brother, who easily equalled his own six-two, pulled on a ludicrously injured expression, which he could still get away with after twenty-four years of perfecting it.

"Well, if you feel that way about it—"

"I do."

Jason sighed. "All right, all right. But I would like to know if you're planning on seeing Taylor again."

"No," Trevor said definitely. "I don't need the complication of a psychic in my life." And thereby, he realized ruefully, he'd tacitly admitted that Taylor had indeed been "the one."

His brother quickly mastered the grin and pulled on yet another in his repertoire of devious faces—this one solemn. "You're not going to see any of them again? You have no curiosity to find out what Solomon's kittens look like or if Jack and Jill escape again or what the significance of that blouse for the Reverend is? You don't want to find out if Jessie actually *does* play the piano and really *isn't* as psychic as the rest of them, or if Dory really *does* hide in closets? You don't want to know if Sara actually *could* topple armies with her eyes or if Luke's really a doctor?"

Trevor stared at him for a moment. Then, in a long-suffering tone, he said, "I always knew it was a curse to have a brother with total recall."

"It helped me a lot in college," Jason confided gravely. "I never had to take notes in class. Now, come on, Trevor, you can't tell me you aren't the least bit curious about that nutty family!"

"Not in the least," Trevor responded, spacing his words for emphasis.

Grinning openly now, Jason said oracularly, "I'll remind you of those words one day, dear brother. One day soon, I think."

* * *

It would have galled Trevor to admit it to his brother, but had Jason been present, he would have gleefully presented his "reminder" the following day.

Trevor didn't realize he was restless at first. He played tennis in the morning with a lawyer friend, had lunch with that same friend afterward, then returned to his apartment, planning on a relaxing afternoon by the pool with a good book. But somehow he never quite got into his suit and out to the pool. He did pick out a book he'd been planning to read for months, but he found himself wandering somewhat aimlessly around with no definite urge to do anything else.

It came to him only gradually, insidiously, that each time he passed his telephone, his hand reached absently for it. Halting by the seductive instrument, Trevor glared at it as if it were a thief caught in the act.

"I'm not interested. I'm just *fine;* no need of psychics in my life. I'm *great . . .* and I am talking to a phone!" He swore irritably. Dropping down into the chair beside the phone, he opened his book and began to read. Tried to read. But something nagged at him, a task needing doing, and he finally reached for the note pad by the phone, jotted down a few numbers with a feeling of relief, then went back to his book.

Half a paragraph later, he set aside his book with careful attention, picked up the pad again, and stared at the phone number he'd unconsciously written down. In one sense, it was not a familiar number; in another sense, it was very familiar. He realized then that at some point during their preparation of dinner the evening before, he had stared fixedly at the kitchen wall phone long enough to memorize Taylor's phone number.

So much for your indifference! he sneered inwardly.

"You've bewitched me!" he told the number severely, picturing a face with vivid blue eyes and fascinating mismatched features. Then he sighed and drew the phone toward him. He wasn't going to get involved, of course. No way. No chance. But he was bored halfway through his vacation, and they *were* an intriguing family . . .

"Hello, Trevor! I knew you'd call and won't you *please* come over because Jack's under the washer again and Daddy's at the office and Solomon's going to show us her kittens I think and Taylor says not to pester you but won't you *please* come? Please?"

It was, of course, the moppet, and Trevor couldn't help but smile. "Hello, Jessie. How'd you know it was me?" He remembered Taylor saying that this sister had the least ability.

"I just knew! Isn't it great?" She sounded happily proud of herself. "I usually can't, you know, but I *did* this time and I think it's 'cause you belong to Taylor or maybe that's not it but anyway *I did*. Can you come, please?"

Trevor bit back a laugh. "Jessie, is Taylor there?"

"Well, she's at the office with Daddy, but I can switch you over."

"Switch me over?"

"To the other phone," Jessie said impatiently. *"This* phone is connected to the one in Daddy's office, which is next door—or something like that. Want me to switch you over?"

"Yes, please," Trevor said meekly.

"Okay—hang on."

There was a short silence filled with a faint buzz, then Taylor's cheerful, efficient voice.

"Doctor Shannon's office."

"Didn't *you* know it was me?" Trevor said severely.

Taylor replied instantly. "Of course. I just wanted to impress you with my businesslike manner."

"Damn."

She giggled. "Sorry, Trevor; it's difficult to surprise a psychic. Did you call the house first?"

"Yes. Jessie switched me over."

"After nattering at you, I'll bet."

"Jack's under the washer again, and Solomon's going to show her kittens," Trevor related automatically. Bemused, he realized that the family had quite definitely infected him with something, and it was spreading rapidly through his bloodstream; he was going to forget how to talk to normal people.

"Well, don't feel obligated. No matter what you think, Trevor, no one's pointing a shotgun at you or readying a matrimonial noose." Her voice was very dry, but amused as well.

Trevor could have argued the point, but wasn't in the mood, for some reason. And he didn't want to think about how utterly comfortable he felt talking to a woman he'd met less than twenty-four hours before. "Well discuss *that* later," he said, sighing as he heard his own admission that there would be a future for them—of some kind. "You work for your father?" he added somewhat hastily.

"Uh-huh. I'm his receptionist this year."

"This year?" he managed blankly.

"Yes, I— Oh, hold on, will you?"

The receiver buzzed in his ear for a few moments; then Taylor was back.

"Sorry, the office is busy today. Why don't you come for dinner? You can go on over to the house; I'll be off in a couple of hours. If you'd like to, that is."

The last diffident sentence got him. "Oh, what the hell. Should I bring something for dinner?"

"Just willing hands," she told him softly, and hung up.

Trevor stared at the receiver in his hand for a moment, then thoughtfully cradled it. With rueful self-mockery, he wondered how on earth a logical, analytical lawyer could have gotten in so deeply over his head.

He continued to wonder about that while he was driving the Jeep out of the city and into the suburb where Taylor lived. But whenever he'd begin to wonder too deeply, a pair of vivid blue eyes would intrude. Trevor finally dispensed with the useless reflection, understanding wryly that neither logic nor analysis was going to produce an answer this time.

Jessie was beside the Jeep almost as soon as it stopped in the drive, and she had Trevor's hand in hers when his feet had barely touched the pavement.

"Oh, I *knew* you'd come! Hurry, Trevor, we have to get Jack before Solomon brings her kittens down and I've practiced a new song—would you like to hear it? You *do* like music, don't you?" She threw the last question anxiously over her shoulder, towing him along behind her like a tiny tugboat pulling a battleship.

Trevor laughed, but something about the moppet

touched him in a way he'd never been touched before. It wasn't just her ridiculous sentences or apparently wild mood swings; he sensed that she needed something from him, something her clearly loving family couldn't provide. And he wondered if Jessie of the "least ability" felt that lack more than her family realized.

He kept his voice casual and friendly when he answered her anxious question, determined to do nothing to set up barriers between himself and the child. "I love music, Jessie; I took piano lessons when I was your age."

Her gray eyes were neither vague like her mother's nor brilliant like her father's, but were distinctively her own: deep smoky pools that brooded one moment and gleamed with a disconcerting wisdom the next. But they flared brilliantly when he claimed some knowledge of music.

"You know music? Really?"

A bit uneasily, Trevor sought to dampen her enthusiasm in the gentlest manner possible. As the side door banged shut behind them, he said carefully, "It was a long time ago, Jessie. I haven't played in years."

"But at least you *know*," she said intensely. "No one else here knows. Oh, they all love music, but they can't play even a note. Not even Daddy, and he has clever hands."

Thoughtfully, Trevor noted that Jessie's sentences became much less tangled when she spoke of music. He filed that knowledge away in his mind as they entered the cheerfully cluttered den and were immediately addressed by Sara, who was sitting between

Jamie and Dory on the couch.

"Jamie closed the laundry room door so Jack can't get out. Hurry and sit down; Solomon wants us to meet her babies."

Pulled firmly down beside Jessie on the love seat, Trevor wondered distantly why no one had thought to close that door yesterday, then silently chastised himself for trying to make sense of anything in this house. But he couldn't help wondering how they could be so sure the cat was about to present her kittens for inspection. Did cats even *do* that?

The Shannon cat did.

She came around the corner just then, ignoring the poodle, which was sitting very still by the doorway. In a measured tread so careful that they could almost hear the music of a march, she entered the room—a tremendous Siamese cat with comically crossed blue eyes and a pure white kitten held securely in her mouth.

Like everyone else, Trevor found himself sitting very still and gazing at the mother and child with respectful eyes. He watched as Solomon gently deposited the kitten on the carpet squarely in the middle of the room, then sat down and gazed—or, at least, appeared to gaze—at Sara.

"How lovely, Solomon," Sara said instantly.

The cat released a peculiarly contented rumble, picked up the kitten, and marched regally from the room. She was back moments later with a kitten, and the little ceremony was repeated.

After she left with the fourth kitten, Trevor could no longer repress a burning question. "How do we know she isn't bringing the same kitten down every time? They're all identical."

Sara's vague eyes focused on him reprovingly. "Of course she isn't, Trevor. A mother knows her children."

Meekly, Trevor watched the fifth repetition of the ceremony. But when the cat had disappeared, he had another question. "Does she do this with every litter?"

"Oh, yes," Sara answered.

"Then why doesn't she wait for the whole family to be here?" Instantly, he felt abashed at the question, telling himself it was ludicrous to suppose the cat could count people or reason. But Sara's answer made his question quite logical and sane by comparison.

"To tease Luke, of course."

"I beg your pardon?" he managed.

"Luke won't let her hide the kittens. He always finds them. So Solomon shows them to the rest of us to get even with him."

"Oh." Trevor decided that there was absolutely nothing he could do with that explanation but accept it. Rather like the way, he reflected, he could only accept his absorption into this ridiculous family.

When Taylor came into the house some time later, she found him in a room off the den, seated in a comfortable chair with Dory nestled confidingly in his lap as they both listened to Jessie play the baby grand piano.

Trevor sent her a quick smile—instantly returned—but said nothing as she came to perch silently on the arm of his chair. And they listened intently as Jessie completed a rather difficult sonata with an expertise belying her young age. As soon as she'd finished, he asked, "D'you compete, Jess?" He'd adopted the diminutive of her name at her request.

She turned on the bench to regard him with bright eyes. "No, never have. I just love to play. D'you . . . think I'm good enough to compete?"

He replied with total honesty. "I went to a West Coast competition last year for kids under eighteen; if you'd competed, you would have won."

Her gray eyes glowed brilliantly at him. "Really?"

"I think you'd have won, Jess. I really do."

Jessie bounded up, excitement lighting her small face. "Taylor, d'you think Mother and Daddy'd let me?"

Taylor was smiling at her. "Why don't you ask them? Mother's digging up flowers out back; Daddy went out there when we came in."

Instantly, her sister raced from the room.

"Digging up flowers?" Trevor queried dryly.

Before she could answer, Dory wiggled from his lap, saying in her gruff little voice, "I want to watch Daddy comb his hair." She looked sternly at Trevor, her hand on his knee. "You won't go away?"

"Not for a while," he said gently, and watched her leave the room before he looked up at Taylor plaintively. "Digging up flowers? And what's that about your father combing his hair?"

She grinned faintly. "It's a little game Mother and Daddy play. At least I think it is, since it's been going on as long as I can remember. The flower bed's Daddy's, you see; he can get anything to grow. And Mother can't tell a flower from a weed until the former's bloomed, which they haven't as yet. So every day during the spring Mother wanders out to the flower bed just before Daddy's due home. And when Daddy comes in and is told by someone—Jamie today—that Mother's in back with a trowel, he lets out an anguished groan and bolts out there to save his flowers."

Fascinated, Trevor said, "What does he say to her?"

"Always the same thing. He takes the trowel away from her very gently and asks if she'd mind fixing him a cup of coffee. Then when she comes into the house, he rakes his hair with both hands—the 'combing' Dory was talking about—and hides the trowel in the garage."

"How's her coffee?" he asked, remembering Sara's ineptitude in the kitchen.

Taylor laughed. "Terrible! Daddy says it's strong enough to raise the dead; he pours it in the flower bed when she isn't looking. It seems to be a dandy fertilizer."

Chuckling, Trevor reached quite unconsciously to pull her down into his lap. "You have a remarkable family, lady."

"Never dull, anyway," she responded, smiling, utterly relaxed in his lap.

He realized then what he'd done. For a moment, he looked bemusedly at their positions, she on his lap and he with one arm around her shoulders and the other lying possessively across her thighs, then closed his eyes for a moment. "I knew it'd happen," he said mournfully.

"What?" she asked, polite, her hands resting on the arm across her thighs.

"I knew you'd entice me into this loony bin!"

"*I* didn't call *you*," she reminded.

"Didn't you?" His voice was rueful. "Now I know how Ulysses felt."

"If you're referring to a siren song, I'll point out that I've never warbled a note in your direction."

"You bewitched me!"

She giggled. "If it makes you feel better to think that."

"It makes me question my sanity slightly less than I would otherwise," he admitted wryly.

"Better bewitched than intelligently unresisting, huh?"

"Bewitched or not, I *am* resisting," he claimed stoutly. "For instance, I am manfully ignoring the ridiculously demure picture you present sitting on my lap wearing a skirt and frilly blouse."

She looked down at herself for a moment, then said thoughtfully, "Yes, you are, aren't you? I'll try for sexy rather than demure next time. Only this, you understand, was for Daddy's patients—not you."

"Oh, of course."

"They wouldn't feel very comfortable with a siren in the office."

"Perfectly understandable." He cleared his throat, deciding it would be better to change the subject. "Speaking of which, you said something on the phone about being your father's receptionist this year?"

Predictably, she didn't need the question to be clarified. "That's right. I've done something different every year since college. The first year, I went to France as—believe it or not—a governess to the young daughter of an American couple who were transferred over there for a year. The second year, I worked as an executive assistant to the manager of an American oil company based in Saudi Arabia. Since then, I've worked here in Chicago—first as a veterinary assistant, then as a private security guard."

Trevor lifted both brows as he gazed at the slender, dainty lady on his lap. "A private security guard?"

"Never judge a lady by her inches," Taylor advised serenely. "Daddy taught me karate as soon as I could walk, and boxing some years later. And since he's an expert marksman and has an excellent collection of guns upstairs in his study, I can handle weapons quite well."

"But a *security guard?*"

"Seemed the thing to do at the time. I like doing different things. As a matter of fact, I'm up for a job in Australia after the first of next year."

"Doing what?"

She grinned. "Assistant to a lawyer. I have some paralegal training."

He lifted only one brow this time. "If you go to Australia," he pointed out, "you can hardly marry me. I don't want to live down under."

"I said I was up for the job, not that I'd accepted it."

"But you'd be bored anyway, living with a dull lawyer like me."

"Oh, I don't know," she said easily. "I'm sure I'd be able to bear up under the strain."

"I work late most nights—"

"I love to read."

"—and take a vacation only every other year—"

"You obviously need a wife to make you take better care of yourself."

Trevor showed her a mock frown. "Right. Just a gentle little woman who could shoot me or throw me over her shoulder if she felt like it."

"My temper's not *very* bad," she explained anxiously.

"I can see it now. I'd be in a bad mood—we all have them, after all—and you'd read my mind and do something rash."

"No, because I'd *know* you were in a bad mood and understand."

"I'd snap at you, and you'd cry."

"There is that," she admitted ruefully. "It'd be just the thing to set me off, too."

Shaking his head, Trevor murmured, "Worser and worser."

"Not exactly traditional wife material, am I?" she mourned.

"Well, you can cook."

Taylor brightened. "I can, can't I? I can sew, too. And I'd never get mad if you brought home someone unexpectedly for dinner."

"You wouldn't?"

"Certainly not. A man's home is his castle."

A little wryly, Trevor said, "But I bet you'd expect me to clean the moat."

She giggled. "No, only mow the lawn and keep the drawbridge oiled. I can change lightbulbs, fix cars, and use a hammer and screwdriver, but I get a bit dizzy on ladders, and lawn mowers don't seem to like me."

"Lawn mowers don't like you? What do they do?"

"They run away with me. Daddy says it's because I forget where the brake is, but I always remember in cars, so I don't think that's it. And they always head for ditches, so I have to bail out."

Trevor blinked. "I see. Anything else I should know? In considering you as wife material. I mean?" He was enjoying the conversation, perhaps because it was filled with such relaxed solemnity.

Taylor considered the question for a moment. "Well, I'd be a dandy asset for a lawyer, because I could tell you in a minute who was guilty. And then there's the fact that you'd never have to explain why you were going to be late for dinner. And we'd never fight over—um—crossed signals, because I'd always know what you *meant,* no matter what you said."

He found himself torn somewhere between fascination and horror. "I'd never be able to call my soul my own!" he objected, half laughing and more than half serious.

"Wouldn't you?" Her arms lifted to encircle his neck, and she smiled at him very gently. "But you'd be able to call my soul yours."

Trevor was having trouble thinking clearly; the soft promises in those vivid blue eyes overpowered everything else. "I . . . could never be as sure about you as you could about me, though," he murmured.

"Then I'll just have to teach you to read my mind."

He realized at that moment that he could read her mind, or at least read the intent in her nakedly honest eyes. "You wouldn't—you little witch," he managed, and he wasn't talking about her teaching him telepathy.

"I wouldn't?" She leaned toward him until their lips were just a whisper away. "Watch me."

Trevor was a strong-willed man and, at times, a stubborn one, but not even the stern inner voice clamoring for self-preservation had the power to keep his arms from encircling her and his lips from responding to hers. And this time he didn't draw away when he felt that incredible warm sense of well-being surrounding him. The insidious warmth lulled him, seduced him, until it blazed suddenly into essential need. His mouth slanted across hers hungrily, demanding what she gave willingly.

"Daddy kisses Mother like that," an interested voice observed.

The intruding voice drew them apart, but reluctantly, and both turned their heads to stare toward the doorway, where Jessie watched them with critical eyes.

"As a matter of fact," she added, "he just kissed her like that in the garden. I think it was because she caught him pouring the coffee on the flowers. But, guess what? They said I could compete if I wanted to! Isn't that *wonderful?* I have to practice!"

Chapter Four

SINCE JESSIE BEGAN at once to practice with fierce concentration, Trevor and Taylor were more or less forced to vacate the room. Taylor went upstairs to change before beginning dinner, while Trevor was gruffly asked by Dory to retrieve the hamster shut up in the laundry room. Jack was safely back in his cage when Taylor returned to the den, and she entered just in time to hear Trevor addressed by her mother.

"Thank you for encouraging Jessie, Trevor," Sara told him in an absent tone. "She never believes us."

"She's very talented," Trevor responded. He listened for a moment to the sounds coming from those talented fingers. "I think you have a virtuoso blooming in there."

"Yes, and so nice for her," Sara said vaguely, then turned to Taylor. "Darling, I got some things for dinner and left them in the kitchen."

"All right, Mother." Taylor didn't wince visibly, but her vivid blue eyes threw a pained, laughing glance at Trevor, explained only when they were alone again in the kitchen.

"The last time Mother 'got some things' for dinner," she told him ruefully, "I found half a steer in the freezer—frozen, of course."

Trevor couldn't help but laugh. "Wonder what she got this time?"

Opening the refrigerator and peering inside, Taylor sighed. "Whatever it is, she didn't put it in here. Now where—"

"Here." Trevor, spotting an anomaly in the neat kitchen, had gone to stand by the back door, where a large metal tub reposed. Gazing bemusedly down at the contents of the tub, he added, "I only hope you know what to do with them."

Taylor joined him. "Oh, no! Lobsters. *Live* lobsters."

"At least they're fresh," he murmured.

From the kitchen doorway, Luke announced, "I'll fix dinner, Taylor, if you'll keep your mother out of the flowers." He was holding a very much alive and indignant lobster in one hand. "One got away," he explained helpfully to them, "so I knew she'd bought lobsters." His benign gaze focused on Trevor. "Taylor hates to cook lobsters, but I'm very good with them. Not allergic to shellfish, are you?"

"No," Trevor managed to answer, ruthlessly swallowing the laugh in his throat.

"Good. Sara was craving them, I expect. She did with Dory. With Jessie it was watermelon, and with Jamie it was peaches. With Taylor—" He looked reproachfully at his eldest daughter. "With Taylor it was truffles. *Truffles!*"

"Sorry, Daddy," Taylor murmured, solemnly taking the blame for her mother's inexplicable long-ago cravings.

"That's all right," he said magnanimously, waving the lobster. "But go guard the flowers now; your mother's looking for the trowel again." Coming the rest of the way into the kitchen, he absently dropped the lobster—pincers waving in mute protest—into the sink and reached for an apron, his vivid blue eyes abstracted. "Now, where did I put the— Oh, there it is."

Taylor caught a fascinated Trevor by the hand and gently pulled him out the back door. "We have to guard the flowers," she reminded him, grave.

Trevor found himself standing in a beautiful yard. It was large for a suburban property, with a neatly trimmed flowering hedge on two sides, several large and graceful oak trees providing plentiful shade, and innumerable rose bushes and flowering plants. There was a hammock strung between two trees near a picnic table, circular whitewashed wooden benches beneath two more oaks, and a dandy playground area in the far corner, complete with swings, slides, tunnels, and everything else a playful childish heart could wish for.

The flower bed was a neat L-shaped affair that conformed to the angles of the house, filled with a riotous growth that hadn't yet bloomed but nonetheless showed vast promise.

There were only two occupants of the yard at the moment: Jamie was stretched out in the hammock, reading a book, and Dory was occupied with a tire swing in the play area.

Trevor pulled his eyes from the serene picture before him and looked down at Taylor. Thinking of the cook busily working in the kitchen, he asked carefully, "Does your father really have patients? People trust him with their bodies?"

Not in the least offended, Taylor giggled. "If you could see him with his patients, you wouldn't have to ask. He's a wonderful doctor, very patient and gentle. And he's all business in the office, not the least bit absurd. I suppose being ridiculous the rest of the time is his way of unwinding."

Trevor shook his head, but made no protest as she pulled him over to sit on one of the benches. "Did he plan this yard?"

"Every bit of it." She gazed off toward the play area, smiling reminiscently. "He built the playground when I was a toddler, and he and Mother would spend hours out there with me. My friends always envied me my parents. They were always ready to drop whatever they were doing to play games or plan a cookout, and they never worried about kids messing up the house or yard. Daddy may panic when Mother gets near his flowers, but he'd never think of scolding a child for trampling on the bed or carelessly uprooting a plant he'd nursed from a seedling."

Staring at her profile as she gazed back over time,

Trevor softly encouraged the memories, no longer avoiding the knowledge that her life was important to him. "What about discipline?"

She laughed quietly. "I don't know if they planned their method—knowing them, probably not!—but it worked. None of us have ever been spanked or grounded or made to stay in our rooms. If we did something wrong, there were never any harsh words. All it took was a frown from Daddy or a hurt look from Mother, and we were honestly contrite. Maybe being psychic had something to do with it, I don't know. The house has always been noisy and cluttered, but there was never an instant's hesitation when a story was demanded or an umpire needed for a neighborhood ball game."

"Lots of love," he murmured.

Taylor nodded. "And plenty to spare. When I was in high school, the Homes for Foreign Students program was popular; at one point we had three foreign kids living with us. Then they started the Student Exchange program, and I spent a school year in London while an English girl lived here." She smiled. "All those kids still write and call Mother and Daddy; they were completely adopted in spirit."

Trevor chuckled. "I'm not surprised. I think I adopted your mother when she approved my name, and your father won me over when he came into the kitchen carrying a lobster."

She smiled up at him. "I always thought my parents were the most fun of anyone I knew. Once some of my friends were sleeping over here—I was about Jamie's age, I think—and they all decided to test my claim that my parents were never upset by anything. So, in the middle of the night, they managed to get two goats into the house. We left the goats in the den and then crept back downstairs to the family room, where we were supposed to be sleeping, all of us giggling and expecting at least one of my parents to be awakened by the noisy goats."

"What happened?"

"Well, the goats were rummaging around above our heads, but we didn't hear anything else and finally went to sleep. The next morning we found Daddy in the kitchen cooking a huge breakfast for us, and he told us quite cheerfully that Mother was in back with the goats—for all the world as if they belonged here. Sure enough, Mother was sitting in the yard, feeding the goats bits of leftovers. When my friends went out there to see with their own eyes, Daddy said to me— in the gentlest way—that since the goats had made something of a mess in the den, perhaps we should clean the room after breakfast. And we did, too. Two of my friends begged me to exchange parents with them," she added, laughing.

"Your parents would be a hard act to follow."

"Idle observation?" she questioned with a smile. "Or are you contemplating parenthood?"

Trevor stared at her for a moment, then said firmly, "I make it a point never to answer loaded questions."

"Really? I'll keep that in mind."

He decided to change the subject. "I thought we were supposed to be guarding the flowers from your mother's fell hand. Where is she?"

"Probably in the garage looking for the trowel," Taylor responded readily, unperturbed. "Heaven only knows what she *will* find, though."

Amused, Trevor was just about to question this cryptic comment when the answer was presented to him by Sara.

"Look what I found," she said, appearing suddenly beside them with her gliding walk. She gazed in vague satisfaction at the object in her hands, which was a somewhat lopsided birdcage constructed of Popsicle sticks. "Is it yours, darling? I can't remember."

"No, Mother, it's Jamie's. She made it in third grade."

"How clever of her."

"What're you going to do with it?" Taylor asked in the tone of one who didn't expect a lucid answer.

And she didn't get one.

"A bird, I suppose," Sara murmured rather doubtfully. "Dory wants one. Or would it break, do you think? Little birds aren't very strong."

"Dory has hamsters," Taylor reminded firmly, "and Solomon doesn't like *them*. She'd definitely eat a bird."

"Would she?" Sara turned her dreamy gray eyes on Trevor. "Do you think she would?"

"Quite likely," he answered gravely.

"Oh. Well, then, I'll put this on the mantle." She smiled gently at him, then spoke to her daughter as she turned away. "I like him much better than that prince who followed you home from Arabia, darling."

"He was a sheik, Mother," Taylor murmured.

"Was he? How nice for him. But tents and things. I'm glad he went away." Serenely, she headed toward the back door.

Trevor stared at his giggling companion. "Sheik?"

Taylor got control of herself and returned his stare solemnly. "Well, yes. I met him while I was working over there."

"And?" Trevor prompted sternly.

She rubbed her nose in a rueful gesture. "And . . . he decided that what he needed was an American wife. He was a very stubborn man, too. When I came back home, he followed me and asked Daddy for my hand."

Choking back a laugh, Trevor said wistfully, "I wish I'd been here to see that. What'd your father say?"

"He told the sheik that since we hadn't any goats or camels for my dowry, he didn't think it would be fair and, besides, he really didn't want me to live so far away for the rest of my life. The sheik started talking about a mansion in Beverly Hills, and Daddy said *that* was too far away and, besides, he didn't trust California not to fall into the ocean."

"Did the sheik give up?"

"Not immediately. Daddy kept pointing out, very gravely, the differences in religion and lifestyle, and the sheik kept promising to change whatever was wrong. Every time Daddy seemed to be cornered, he found a new objection. Finally, he told the sheik that he really didn't want to lose his firstborn just yet."

"And?"

Taylor grinned up at him. "And then Jamie walked into the room. My fickle sheik instantly fell in love with her and offered Daddy the earth if he'd only consent to their marriage. He was horribly disappointed when he found out how old she was, but he stayed for dinner anyway, and when he left he promised he'd be back to court Jamie in a few years."

Passing by them just then, Jamie said softly, "I hope he does come to court me. He was a beautiful man, Taylor, and *such* nice manners. And I'd like to ride a camel. And at least he didn't yell like that Frenchman." With a gliding walk eerily like her mother's, Jamie moved on toward the house.

Trevor folded his arms across his chest and leaned against the tree at his back, staring down at Taylor. "Frenchman?" he queried with terribly polite patience.

She was gazing meditatively at nothing at all. "Hmm? Oh, him. He was just someone I met in Paris."

"He followed you back to the States?"

"Uh-huh."

"And asked for your hand?" Trevor's voice was growing more and more polite.

"Well, yes."

"And?"

Taylor sent him a sudden, glinting smile. "Judging by your tone, I think you would have loved Daddy's answer."

"Only," Trevor said grimly, "if he decked the man."

"He did."

"He did?"

She giggled. "Well, I'm afraid he took Daddy's amiability for weakness, and he became very demanding and—uh—abusive. And when he began shouting and frightening Dory, Daddy knocked him down. I must say it worked, too, because he begged pardon very meekly once he'd picked himself up off the floor, and he left without a murmur."

Trevor was clearly pleased by his mental image of

that event, but he held on to his stern expression. "Do you make it a habit of bringing strange men home with you?" he asked severely.

"You should know," she told him blandly.

Without an instant's hesitation he said, "But you knew I was the man you were going to marry. What excuse did you have for the others?"

She choked on a giggle. "You make it sound like I've had men trampling a beaten path to my door!"

"I'm beginning to think that was exactly the case! I thought you waited for me!" he accused, aggrieved.

"A girl has to do *something* while she waits," Taylor explained gently.

"You shameless hussy, how many other men have you brought home?"

"Not many."

"Not many?"

She looked up at him soulfully. "And you're the only one who *mattered,* after all."

"Oh, sure!"

"I promise. It's just that I like making friends, you see."

Trevor made a rude noise. "Friends who propose?"

"Well, only three proposed—" She broke off abruptly with a comical look of guilty dismay.

"Three? And just who was the third?"

Taylor sighed. "Well, he was a man I met in—"

"Let me guess," Trevor interrupted in a voice of foreboding. "Just a man you met in London?"

She nodded, half laughing and half guilty. "But I was a schoolgirl, after all, so it didn't really count."

"You," he told her firmly, "should be barred from

world travel! It's obvious you make a habit of en-
snaring strange foreign men. I shudder to think of
what you'd bring home from Australia."

Meditatively, she said, "I was planning on Italy
after Australia."

Trevor fought with himself for a silent moment,
then said calmly, "You'll probably catch a doge or a
count over there. *Much* better than a stodgy American
lawyer."

She started to laugh. "Damn! I hoped you'd take
the bait!"

He lifted a superior brow at her. "And find myself
engaged because I'd gone all primitive and possessive
and ordered you not to go anywhere?"

"It was just a thought," she explained wistfully.

Manfully ignoring her pensive smile and mournful
eyes, he said sternly, "Well, it won't work!"

"You'd let me go off to Australia with that other
lawyer?"

"It's none of my business where you go," he said.

"You wouldn't lift a finger to stop me?"

"Not a finger."

"You wouldn't even *ask* me not to go?"

"It's none of my business," he repeated stoutly.

She stared at him for a moment, sad. Then, before
his startled and horrified gaze, large tears pooled in
the vivid blue eyes and rolled silently down her cheeks.

"Taylor!" Shaken, he took her hands in his and was
just about to apologize fervently for making her cry.
Then he remembered how easily she claimed to cry,
and suspicion narrowed his eyes.

Slowly, she began to smile, amusement gleaming

behind the tears. "You remembered. I wondered if you would."

"You—witch!" He released her hands and pulled out his handkerchief. "Here. Wipe those crocodile tears," he ordered.

She did so, still smiling as she handed the cloth back to him. "Well, it was worth a try," she confessed cheerfully.

"Can you always *make* yourself cry?"

"Oh, yes—except when I'm really upset. For instance, if you really did let me go off to Australia, I wouldn't cry at all. I wouldn't be able to," she said simply.

Trevor fought a desire to promise he wouldn't let her leave the country, ruefully aware of what would most likely happen if she *did* leave. "I'd probably chase after you anyway," he muttered.

"Would you?" She seemed entranced by the idea.

He stared at her for a moment, then reached out and hugged her. Hard. "Damn you," he said a bit thickly.

Taylor smiled up at him when his embrace loosened enough to allow her to do so. "I'm going to go on chasing you, you know," she said confidingly. "I know a good thing when I find one. And I have a slight advantage over most women."

"Which is?" he asked wryly.

"An unconventional upbringing. And a psychic certainty that we'll be married someday. So with me, it's no holds barred."

"I believe I've said it before," he murmured, "but a sane man would run like hell."

"I don't see you taking to your heels," she observed.

Abruptly, Luke stuck his head out the back door and waved a ladle at them. "If you want dinner," he called to them, harassed, "you'll come get your mother out of the kitchen, Taylor! She's got a birdcage. Why does she have a birdcage when we don't have any birds? And Jamie's sitting on the counter reading out loud, and I've lost a lobster—" The door banged shut on his last comment as Luke disappeared back inside.

Trevor rose to his feet, pulling her up with him. "Did I say a sane man would run? Well, it's obvious why I'm not running. Only an *insane* man would get involved with this ridiculous family," he said whimsically.

It was late before Trevor got home that night, mainly because Luke had instigated a poker game after the lobster had been consumed. They'd played for fantastic sums, and after losing every hand to one or another of the family, Trevor declared that he'd never again play cards with psychics.

But he thoroughly enjoyed the evening.

Sometime during the wee hours of the morning, alone and sleepless in his bed, it occurred to Trevor that if he wanted to preserve his unattached status, he'd better stay as far as possible from Taylor and her nutty but curiously attractive family. Instead of counting sheep, he kept repeating that to himself over and over, until sleep finally claimed him.

The end result was that Trevor kept himself fiercely occupied for the next three days. He played tennis and, if that didn't tire him physically, swam endless laps in the pool and even jogged every morning. He defeated his brother soundly at handball, all the while turning a deaf ear to Jason's innocent, persistent questions about Taylor. And at night, he buried himself in every literary potboiler he could lay his hands on until his tortured mind demanded sleep.

Jason said little about his brother's deliberately hectic vacation until the third night, when he came over to Trevor's apartment for pizza and a televised baseball game. The game was in the second inning when Trevor called to order the pizza, and when he hung up the phone, he saw that his brother was thumbing bemusedly through the latest potboiler.

Deadpan, Jason gazed at the lurid cover, then lifted shocked eyes to Trevor's face. "Your taste in literature's gone downhill these last few days," he remarked critically.

Ignoring this, Trevor said, "You start your vacation next week, don't you?" Jason worked as an electrical engineer with a large construction company.

"Yep. And, unlike you, I don't plan to fritter away my days off by exercising until I can't move or reading lousy books until I can't think. I'm flying to Wyoming, where I plan to spend a leisurely week hiking and fishing."

Jason's tone had been perfectly bland, but it caused Trevor to feel suddenly sheepish. "Is that what I've been doing?" he murmured.

"Yes," his brother told him cordially.

Trevor shifted a bit uncomfortably on the couch. "Look, it's *my* vacation," he said defensively.

"Of course it is. And who am I to say you're driving yourself into an early grave? I'm only your little brother. You're older, after all. Presumably wiser. Presumably, you know what you're doing. Now, if you *were* to ask my opinion, I'd just have to wonder why it is that you seem to be working so damned hard to get through your vacation. It's almost as if you want to be too tired to think. As if you're afraid to let yourself think—"

"All right! I get the point."

But Jason wasn't finished. Coolly, he said, "It isn't like you, brother. You've never been one to avoid facing whatever's bothering you. Or *who*ever." He hesitated, then added bluntly, "You faced up to the fact that you and Kara should never have gotten engaged."

Trevor said nothing, only frowned at the television.

Jason sent a searching glance at his brother's closed face. "But maybe that was different," he ventured quietly. "Maybe it didn't bother you then because you didn't care enough. Maybe it bothers you now because you care too much. She's gotten under your skin, hasn't she?"

"Where'd you get your degree in psychology?" Trevor countered with taut sarcasm.

Even more quietly, Jason said, "I got it from watching the brother who raised me while he was putting himself through college and law school."

Trevor's frown vanished. After a moment, he glanced at Jason and said gruffly, "Sorry, Jase."

Jason grinned a little in response. "Well, it isn't really any of my business. But I can't help thinking

that since I loused up your last serious relationship—"

"What the hell are you talking about?"

It was Jason's turn to be uncomfortable, but he met
Trevor's suddenly grim eyes squarely. "Kara didn't
make any secret of it at the time: She didn't want a
sixteen-year-old kid living with her. And who could
blame her?"

Trevor turned on the couch until he was facing his
brother, no longer making any pretense of watching
the ball game. "Jase, we didn't break up because of
you."

"I was a part of the reason, though," Jason said
steadily.

Because they'd always been honest with each other,
Trevor hesitated only a second. "In a way. Because I
wasn't about to let my brother go live with some
distant relative. But that isn't why we broke up, Jase.
It just made me realize I could never be happy living
with Kara."

Jason nodded but said, "I—used to worry about
that. Blame myself."

Reaching out to grip his shoulder, Trevor said firmly,
"Don't."

"Well, actually, I talked myself out of that pretty
quickly," Jason admitted ruefully. "I never liked Kara."

Trevor laughed and shook his brother's shoulder
briefly before releasing him. With the atmosphere
eased, Jason instantly took advantage of it.

"And since we're discussing the women in your
life, I'll go on being nosy. Are you going to come
clean with me about Taylor?"

Trevor grimaced faintly. He stared at nothing in particular for a moment, then sighed. "What can I say about a woman who tells me—scant minutes after we meet—that she's the woman I'm going to marry?"

Jason blinked. "What? Straight-out like that?"

"Straight-out like that." Reflectively, he added, "Taylor doesn't pull her punches. She's quite possibly the most honest woman I've ever met in my life."

"Oh. Well, uh—what's wrong with that?"

Trevor stared at him. "She can read my mind any time she damn well feels like it."

Jason hid a grin behind the hand thoughtfully rubbing his face. "That . . . could be a drawback in a relationship," he admitted.

"And her family," Trevor continued, rueful, "may be sane, but if so, it's only by the skin of their collective teeth."

Jason choked. Controlling himself beneath his brother's pained eye, he finally managed to speak. "You went back and saw them that next day, didn't you?"

"Yes. I got the hamster out from under the washer again and encouraged Jessie to compete at the piano. Dory sat in my lap, and they all won imaginary money from me at poker. Sara got lobsters for dinner—live lobsters, which Luke prepared—but two got away and it took ten minutes to find the second one."

Fascinated, Jason asked, "And Taylor?"

"Taylor?" Trevor cleared his throat. "Well, Taylor told me some things about her life, including the information that she's worked in a different job every year since college. And sometimes a different country.

A sheik followed her home from Saudi Arabia; a Frenchman followed her home from Paris; and an Englishman proposed to her in London."

"She told you that?"

"Only under duress, so to speak. Sara brought up the sheik; she likes me better than him, because of tents and things. Jamie compared the sheik favorably to the Frenchman, who yelled. And Taylor accidently mentioned the Englishman."

"Did she offer an excuse for bringing home foreign men?" Jason asked solemnly.

"She likes making friends."

After a moment, Jason said carefully, "Don't bite my head off, but—uh—do you believe that *was* her reason?"

"Oh, yes. She's honest, you see. There isn't a doubt in my mind that Taylor hasn't had a serious relationship with a man in her life." Meditatively, he added, "She was waiting for me."

"Knowing you'd come along eventually?"

"Don't run away with the idea that she was waiting for Prince Charming," Trevor urged dryly. "It's just that she's psychic; she was always sure she'd know the right man when she met him."

"And you're the right man."

"So she says."

"Which is why you've spent the past few days carefully ignoring her existence?"

Trevor sighed, then said ruefully, "D'you know, I hadn't been in that house ten minutes before everyone assumed I belonged to Taylor? Luke said he wouldn't have organ music at the wedding. Jamie asked me innocently if I belonged to Taylor, and Dory *told* me I did after she touched my shoulder. As far as they're concerned, the wedding's only a formality." He stared at his brother. "D'you blame me for running?"

Before Jason could answer, the doorbell rang. Trevor went to answer it, remembering the pizza he'd ordered. But when he opened the door, he found a delivery man with an armful of something that definitely wasn't pizza.

"Trevor King?" the man queried, shifting his load to peer around it.

"Yes?"

A tremendous basket of long-stemmed red roses was thrust into Trevor's startled arms, and the delivery man said cheerfully, "These are for you; she must be crazy about you, pal!" Then he was gone.

Bemused, Trevor closed the door and carried the basket into the den, where he set it on the coffee table.

"There's a card," Jason offered gravely.

The card, opened, revealed a few lines Trevor recognized as a paraphrase from a work of George Bernard Shaw.

You believe it is your part to woo, to persuade, to prevail, to overcome, but you're the pursued.

The card wasn't signed. But then, it hardly needed to be.

Trevor knew he was smiling but couldn't seem to stop himself. "Damn that little witch," he murmured, and felt no surprise when the words bore a closer resemblance to a caress than to a curse.

Chapter Five

TWO DAYS LATER, with only a weekend left of his vacation, Trevor finally gave in and called Taylor. She answered the phone herself, and he wasted no time identifying himself; it was needless, he knew.

"Thank you for the flowers," he told her gravely.

"You're welcome," she said, equally solemn. "I hope you like roses."

"I like roses. I also liked the gardenias yesterday and the box of chocolates today. My entire apartment building is intrigued."

"Did I embarrass you?"

"Would it disturb you if I said yes?"

"Not particularly."

"I didn't think so."

Taylor laughed. "How does it feel to be pursued?"

"I haven't made up my mind yet." Trevor paused. "But my brother says he's in love with you."

"A man of obvious taste."

"No, just a radical sense of humor."

"Thanks a lot!"

Trevor laughed, but the sound held a sigh. "Taylor, you are not making this easy for me."

"That's supposed to be the lady's line," she said blandly.

"Tell me about it!"

"Well, if you want to fight about it, why not come to dinner and we'll fight over the pasta. You love Italian food," she added enticingly.

Trevor told himself quite firmly that he accepted this guileless invitation only because he was convinced the days away from Taylor and her family had put things rigidly into perspective. He told himself he was utterly and completely convinced of that.

Jason would have laughed uproariously.

So Trevor, after five days in which to put "things" into perspective, once again ventured a foray into Taylor's absurd family. He kept a close guard on himself, taking care to avoid being alone with Taylor for any length of time because he was determined to let nothing irrevocable happen between them.

He spent the better part of the weekend with the family, and even though he was ruefully aware that Taylor was amused by his guardedness, he couldn't help but enjoy himself.

He found himself giving Luke a hand with the

gardening, listening to Jessie practicing on the piano, reading to Dory, and helping Jamie groom the family poodle, Agamemnon. It became a ritual to help Taylor with the preparation of meals for the family. And Sara more than once requested his help in various bizarre chores he thought prudent not to question, such as looking all through the attic for an ancient pair of ballet slippers. And hunting through various closets for a hat with feathers. What she did with both his finds Trevor didn't dare ask, although he saw neither again.

Given the run of the house and the unshadowed trust of the family, Trevor grew far more comfortable than his self-preserving inner voice liked. Since no one displayed further evidence of ESP—even Taylor, if she read his thoughts, kept quiet about it—he was able to put from his mind the knowledge that this family was unusual in more than just behavior and personality. He was even beginning to understand them.

Luke, for all his softly hurried style of speech and all the "chaff mixed in with the grain," as Taylor ruefully described it, possessed a brilliant mind and a cool composure in emergencies. Trevor discovered the latter when Dory fell from a tree in the backyard on Sunday morning. Everyone was anxious, though all were calm, and Luke was gently expert in examining the sprained ankle of his youngest daughter while she sat in Trevor's lap. Trevor had to remind himself that this man was a doctor with quite a few years of practice behind him. The brilliant mind was discovered while they weeded and pruned in the backyard, when several of Luke's low and somewhat hurried remarks and questions forced Trevor to dredge into memories of college courses just to hold his own with the man.

He also, more than once, caught a gleam of laughter in Luke's vivid but benign eyes, and slowly realized that Taylor had been right: Her father very consciously used absurdity to unwind. His was a very demanding profession, and a serious one; obviously, laughter was Luke's way of dealing with that. And since every member of his family lovingly played their ridiculous parts, it was an easy and natural thing for him to do.

As for Sara, Trevor discovered to his own wry satisfaction that his court-sharpened senses had not been at fault: She was *definitely* not as vague as she appeared and acted. He came unexpectedly into the den on Saturday afternoon to find her engrossed in a book. That in itself seemed unusual enough, because Sara rarely sat, obviously preferring to wander about in the yard or house with a vague and fleeting interest in just about everything. But it was the title of the book that caught Trevor's astonished eyes, and long moments passed before it sunk into his brain that she was reading philosophy.

Clearly feeling a startled stare—or, for all he knew, feeling it telepathically—she lifted her eyes to meet his. In her vivid gray eyes was the intelligence he'd seen only once before, and in back of that was a rueful smile.

"You went to college," he said firmly, as if she were going to argue with him.

"Between babies," she answered sedately.

Suspicious, he demanded, "Phi Beta Kappa?"

Her smile was as sweet and vague as ever, but the vividness didn't leave her eyes. She nodded. Marking her place in the book with one slender finger, she rose to her feet. "Do you really think, Trevor," she said tranquilly, "that a stupid woman could have kept up with Luke all these years?"

"Not stupid," he protested.

"Just not all here?" She laughed softly at his bemusement. "But it's so dull being just like everyone else," she murmured. "And so boring for the children. We laugh at ourselves, you know, and most families can't." Her eyes were vague again. "That hat with the feathers. So pretty on the wall. I'll have to find a place for it somewhere."

"Sara—" he managed as she was turning away.

"Yes, Trevor?"

He sighed. "Nothing."

Her eyes gleamed at him briefly. "It so often is." She wandered away.

Trevor could hardly help but laugh. He shook his head and left the room, still laughing.

Of the other members of the family, he also discovered a great deal. Dory, the pixie, was a stoic physically but timid in her emotions; she clung to him often in a way that gripped at his heart, but she was gruff in speech and tended to hide herself away from curious eyes if she was upset. She was obviously secure in her family's love but insecure in herself. She clearly considered Trevor a part of the family and treated him like an adored older brother. And she talked to him with vast seriousness, even confiding, as he was reading to her, why she hid in closets.

"I like the dark. It's quiet."

Touched, he said gently, "Is it loud everywhere else, Dory?"

She reflected gravely, those brilliant, solemn eyes meeting his directly. "Sometimes. In my head. Taylor says I'll learn to close the door in my head and not need a closet. Sometimes I can. But sometimes I can't, so I go into the closet."

"I'm sure Taylor's right," he said, inwardly uncertain.

A shy, fleeting smile crossed Dory's face. "You keep your door closed a lot," she observed. "Did you learn when you were little like me?"

Trevor thought he understood. "I'm different from the rest of you, honey. I don't have to close a door because I don't need one. I can't—*hear* things the way you can."

Peering intently at him, Dory laughed suddenly, an odd, gruff little laugh. "You don't know."

Puzzled, he asked, "Know what?"

But Dory said no more on the vague subject, just smiled at him with curious wisdom and requested that he finish the story.

Baffled, Trevor had the elusive feeling that he should have understood her—and hadn't somehow.

It was just one more puzzle piece fitting nowhere.

Jamie, that serene wraith, saw everything—like her mother—and possessed the most even temperament Trevor had ever known; she was neither uncaring nor controlled, but simply calm and serene. She was sweet and confiding, never bored or restless. She was the seamstress of the family, willingly putting aside something else to mend a tear or sew on a button. In looks, she was the feminine image of her father except for dreamy gray eyes, and she had something of his soft, hurried style of speech. And, emotionally, of all the daughters she seemed the closest to her father.

Talking to Trevor casually, she told him that Luke hoped the fifth Shannon child would be another girl.

"Does he?" Trevor asked with a smile, thinking how tranquil her Madonna-like serenity was.

"Oh yes. He says he's had so much fun with girls, and girl babies are so sweet."

"Doesn't he know if it'll be a girl?" Trevor asked curiously, having already discovered that each of the daughters was utterly-matter-of-fact about their psychic abilities.

Jamie giggled suddenly. "He always guesses the sex of his patients' babies, but he never can with Mother's. He says she hides it from him. The rest of us are sure it's a girl, but Mother won't say, and she's the only one who really *knows.*"

Trevor recalled Taylor's remark about it being difficult to surprise a psychic. Another one of Sara's gently humorous games? he wondered.

With the Shannon family . . . who knew?

Jessie, the moppet, was temperamental, moody; she fought her way through highs and lows with equal energy and boasted incredible determination in her slender, tomboyish form. His own love and understanding of music had made him something of a demigod in Jessie's eyes, and she talked to him without any of the emotional emphasis she used with everyone else.

"D'you really think I'm good enough, Trevor?"

"You've got talent, Jess, real talent."

She smiled blindingly at him. "I'm glad you came here to belong to Taylor. I knew the mailman was coming this morning before he came around the corner, and I passed Jamie the salt before she asked for it. I didn't think I was psychic at all until you came."

"Not everybody's psychic, Jess," he reminded gently. "I'm not."

"You're not?"

"No."

Jessie frowned at him. "You're sure?"

"Very sure," he answered, amused.

She gave him a rather odd look, he thought, but seemed to accept his assurances.

He wondered, though.

And Taylor... Taylor. She grew more beautiful every time Trevor looked at her, her chestnut hair more vibrant, her candid blue eyes more vivid, her mismatched features more fascinating and alluring. She was intelligent, humorous, tolerant. She was, both ostensibly and actually, the briskly capable hub around which her peculiar family turned. Viewing her family with love and respect, she was nonetheless ruefully aware of their oddity and entirely tolerant of it. And she was the most honest woman he'd ever met.

He knew why men would be attracted to her; her beauty was certainly a part of it, but those eyes, those honest eyes... And since he knew well that the intelligence of American men was at least equal to that of foreign ones, he didn't doubt that men had been following Taylor around for years. He wondered about those others but didn't ask. He felt no conceit in the sure knowledge that only male friends preceded him, but he felt a strong responsibility in the knowledge that he had the power to hurt her, and hurt her badly.

He didn't consider his careful guardedness as nobility. He knew only that until he was as sure as she was, their relationship would remain platonic and feelings undeclared. And there was still a niggling unease in the back of his mind, a stout wall closing off a part of himself from her.

That vague, nebulous uncertainty assumed concrete form on Sunday evening. He and Taylor were, for once that day, alone. They were in the den, engrossed in a chess game. The board was before them on the coffee table, and both sat forward, elbows on knees, Taylor frowning over his last move.

"I think you've trapped me," she complained.

"Never say die," he advised her.

"Well, I won't concede anyway," she said, and reached out to make a brilliant move.

Trevor blinked. "Damn."

She giggled.

The phone rang out in the hall just then; both of them ignored it as they stared down at the board, Trevor taking his turn to frown.

Moments after the phone rang, Luke appeared in the doorway to say quietly, "It's Dave, Taylor. He says it's important."

She didn't get up and head for the phone, but instead gazed at her father for a long, unreadable moment. "All right, Daddy," she said finally in a low voice. "Tell him to come over."

Luke nodded and went back into the hall.

Trevor looked at her in puzzlement. She seemed suddenly a bit tense, a bit preoccupied. "I realize it's none of my business," he said, "but who's Dave?" He thought she wasn't going to answer, which was so oddly unlike her that it made him anxious—inexplicably, he told himself fiercely—about this unknown man. But then she did answer.

"Dave is a senior detective in the homicide division."

"A cop?"

"A very good one." Taylor sighed, and to the watching man, her eyes seemed abruptly older than they had any right to be. "A few years ago his sister, who's a friend of mine, told him he should ask me for help in a homicide case. He was broad-minded enough to appreciate the fact that police departments have used psychics in the past, and he was by no means too proud to ask for help."

"So you helped him."

She nodded. "On the understanding that my name wouldn't be mentioned anywhere. Not in his official reports and not to the press. He felt guilty about that when I was able to tell him where he could find the killer and then he got all the credit. But we had a long talk and straightened everything out. By now, he understands how I feel about it."

"And how do you feel?" Trevor asked, curiously.

Taylor looked at him with those too-old eyes and smiled faintly. "It isn't a pleasant thing to look into the mind of a killer; I couldn't handle that along with the attention the press would focus on me. I feel a responsibility to do what I can to help—but on my own terms. I won't be held up to the public as some kind of freak, and I won't have the police department ridiculed because they ask a psychic to help them."

Before Trevor could say anything—not that there was anything he *could* say—Luke came back into the room.

"He was calling from his car; he'll be here in a minute."

Taylor nodded silently. Trevor, watching her intently, realized that she'd somehow withdrawn into herself. And he wondered what it did to this sensitive, cheerful woman to look into the mind of a killer.

The rest of the family drifted in soon thereafter. They all seemed unusually subdued, and it took Trevor some moments to realize that they would remain near Taylor during whatever was to come, supporting her emotionally. And the silence of the normally talkative family disturbed him more than anything else.

Luke went to answer the summons of the doorbell, returning with a tall man in his mid-thirties who had graying black hair and intelligent brown eyes. As he was introduced to the detective, Trevor saw that his eyes were also very weary. Dave Miller sat down in a chair at right angles to Taylor and, though his lean face was unexpressive, he was clearly distressed.

"I'm sorry about this, Taylor. But we're at a standstill, nothing to go on, and if this creep follows the pattern he's established . . . Random killings, nothing to tie the victims together, not a damn thing we can hold on to—"

"It's all right, Dave." She smiled at him, calm, quiet. "What've you got?"

From his pocket, the detective produced a plastic bag containing a black glove that bore ominous rusty stains on the fingers. He carefully rolled the top of the bag down so that it was possible to touch the material without touching the stains. "This didn't belong to the latest victim, but it was found near the body. If it's his—"

Taylor reached out to take the bag from him, her fingers closing over the exposed material. She fingered it for a moment in silence, then suddenly went deathly pale. The bagged glove dropped to the floor.

"Taylor?" Trevor wanted to reach out and hold her suddenly, but he feared to break her concentration or somehow further disturb her with unwanted interference.

She sent him a reassuring if strained smile and bent to pick up the glove again. "It belongs to the killer," she murmured almost inaudibly. Obviously unwilling to ask it of her, Dave nonetheless spoke gently. "Can you tell me where to look for him?"

A pulse was beating strongly in Taylor's neck, but her pale face was calm. She closed her eyes and sat for long minutes holding the glove. Then her eyes opened—feverishly bright eyes, Trevor noted in alarm—and she dropped the stained thing on the coffee table beside their unfinished chess game. Her hands rubbed against her jean-clad thighs in the unconscious gesture of wiping away dirt.

Huskily, she said, "There's an apartment building on the east side of town. An old one. The fire escape faces the street. And there's a windowbox with—with geraniums: second floor, corner apartment. I think he's in that apartment. I know he's in that building. It's somewhere near Maple Street."

The detective picked up the glove and returned it to his pocket, nodding. "I know the area. Taylor . . . thank you."

"Just get him, Dave." Her eyes were still feverishly bright. "Get him before he can do that again."

He rose to his feet. "I'll call and let you know."

Luke and Sara walked him to the front door, and Trevor only dimly realized that the others had also left the room; all his attention was focused on the white, stricken face and glittering eyes of the woman sitting stiffly, controlled, at his side.

"Taylor?"

She looked at him blindly, trapped somehow in a dark place of little creeping things and big stomping ones. "Why is it," she said in a reasonable, matter-of-fact tone, "that I can't cry when it matters? I wish it was the other way around. I wish I could cry when it mattered and not when it didn't."

Instinctively, Trevor reached out to enfold her in his arms, holding her rigid body in a comforting embrace. He said nothing, but only held her. A part of his mind noted that there was no "security blanket" this time, and that same distant piece of his intelligence realized that it was because she was rigidly locked inside herself. Not, he knew, because she didn't trust him with her vulnerability, but because, for her, there had never been an outlet for this kind of emotion.

"Why you?" he demanded, unconsciously fierce. "Why do you have to do this?"

In that same toneless, matter-of-fact voice, she said,

"Because I'm the strongest. Stronger even than Mother or Daddy. It wouldn't be so bad if—if I could only *cry.*"

The same dim part of his mind that saw so clearly and made him uncomfortable with what it saw spoke up now softly in his mind. And it sneered at him because he wouldn't recognize the fact that *he* could be her outlet for this painful, imprisoned emotion. With the best and most loving will in the world, her family couldn't help; she was a woman, and a woman would share the vulnerable part of her self only with the man she gave her heart to. *They* could see her pain but were helpless to ease it; *he* could see her pain— and refused to.

Holding her, feeling the stiffness of her body, Trevor fought a violent inner battle. The wall that stood between them was his, a conscious thing, and he knew now why he couldn't remove it.

She could read his mind.

So simple. He was an intelligent man; he knew why that very simple statement—fact—disturbed him so deeply. It was a human need to be seen, to be known, but it was equally important to be able, when necessary, to retreat into the privacy of one's own silent thoughts. And that primitive part of his mind shied violently from the knowledge that with Taylor there would be no solitude.

That was what belonging to Taylor really meant.

And guilt caused his arms to tighten around her as that dim sneering voice proclaimed that with him . . . she would be able to cry when it mattered. If the wall were down. If they loved.

He felt it, then, when that wall rose higher. And he felt something that might have been hope shrivel. Holding her motionless body tightly, he said, "You're tired. You should sleep." He was surprised at the even tone of his voice.

She pushed gently away from him, her face calm now, but the wonderfully honest eyes still curiously blind. "No. I'll have nightmares," she added simply. "I always do." She looked at their unfinished chess game, then smiled at him. "It's your move."

Truer than you know, he thought bleakly. Then, because he could do nothing else for her, he leaned forward to resume the game.

It was a couple of hours later when he rose to leave. Her eyes were no longer blind but calm and quiet. She said good night in something approaching her normal cheerful voice. But Trevor ached for her.

During the drive into the city to his apartment he fought inwardly, knowledge against desire, disquiet against the urge to at least *try.* If he could be sure that he was indeed the man for her—but he couldn't be sure. His emotions rioted until he didn't know what he felt.

He found a backpack just inside his front door and hoped his face was equal to Jason's perceptive eyes. His brother was lying on the couch, the room lit only by the glow of the television.

With an engaging grin, Jason said, "Your place is closer to the airport, and I have an early plane in the morning. D'you mind?"

"No, I don't mind. You've slept here before."

Abruptly, Jason sat up and turned on the lamp beside him, his green eyes fixed keenly on his brother's face. Oddly hesitant, he said, "I don't have to leave tomorrow, you know. I can stick around for a few days."

"Why should you do that?" Trevor asked, surprised.

"Just . . . in case you want to talk."

"I go back to work tomorrow, remember?" Trevor wondered vaguely what his brother saw in his face to cause that younger face to go suddenly grim. "I'm fine."

"Are you?"

Pausing on his way toward the bedroom, Trevor looked levelly at Jason. "I'm fine. And you'll get on that plane if I have to put you on it myself. See you in the morning, Jase."

"Good night."

Trevor got ready for bed, sparing only a brief moment for a look in his dresser mirror. He didn't see anything in his own calm face, but it occurred to him as he slid between the sheets that he looked older than he'd thought.

In the morning, Jason said nothing more about deferring his vacation, but his eyes on Trevor were searching and troubled. Trevor noticed, but he said nothing. He put his brother safely on his plane and then went on to the law firm where he was a junior partner.

His work kept him busy, occupied. His attaché case loaded with briefs and notes, he worked long into the night at home. In the office he buried himself in legal tomes and made short, curt work of telephone calls. In court, one beaten prosecutor congratulated him on his coldly brilliant defense of his client, and another asked ruefully if he'd mind very much changing sides because the prosecutor's office could use some wins.

It wasn't until the end of the week that Trevor realized his secretary was creeping warily around him and speaking with unusual softness. Aware at last, he also saw that the entire staff was casting nervous looks his way.

He spent Friday afternoon with his hands folded atop his desk and his gaze focused on nothing. Thinking. For an even-tempered man to unsettle his entire office with his moodiness, his personal problems spilling over into his professional responsibilities, was unthinkable. But Trevor was not, as Jason had observed, a man who could long avoid facing up to problems.

D'you think you've forgotten her, fool? You know damned well you're being cowardly in not facing her. Cowardly in not telling her what's wrong. She got under your skin that first day, she and her ridiculous family. Got under your skin with those nakedly honest eyes. You don't want to hurt her. Even if you know you can't live with her. Because, for the two of you, it's going to take more than . . . love.

Trevor heard a ragged sigh escape into the silent room. He loved her. Another . . . simple . . . unquestionable . . . unbearable fact. He loved her, but he wasn't the man for her. The man for Taylor wouldn't feel this need to hide a part of himself from her.

The man for Taylor could laugh with her.

He wouldn't hide from her, Trevor silently answered to the silent voice in his mind.

He'd have to love that ridiculous family of hers.

Any man would love them.

She has honest eyes, the voice reminded stingingly.

Trevor sighed again. Honest eyes. An honest heart—and God only knew if she loved him; believing they'd marry "one day" was hardly a declaration of love. And if she did love him, what then?

He could hurt her so badly.

And hurt himself. He was already hurting, wasn't he? Wasn't that why he'd been biting the heads off his staff, why he'd been cold and decisive with everyone he'd spoken to? Why he'd brusquely shunned his brother's ready sympathy, turned a deaf ear to that willing one?

It occurred to him then that he, in his pain, had shut out everyone. Just as Taylor shut herself in with the pain her gift brought to her. Was that the real reason he'd ached for her pain? Because it reminded him of his own inability to share his pain with another?

The breakup with Kara—Jason had known, but they'd not discussed it then, and there had been no one else to talk to. Before that, the deaths of their parents in a plane crash, the tearing grief and shock. The struggle to raise a much-loved brother and take the place of two parents. The struggle of college and law school.

Except for the deaths of his parents, he regretted none of it. But it hadn't been easy.

Automatically, Trevor opened his attaché case and piled papers into it. Still thinking.

He was a lawyer, accustomed to looking for what-ever would benefit his client. Bits and pieces, legal loopholes, careful maneuvering, an obscure precedent in a dusty book. Digging for the best out of a witness.

Now he was his own client. And dig though he had, he kept coming up against the wall in himself. He could willingly share a great deal with Taylor, but not the last dark corner of his mind. Not that place where old hurts were deeply buried alongside old fears and inevitable guilts. Not that place every sane mind needs apart from the rest where gremlins lurked in the dark.

He couldn't share that with her.

Trevor went home to a silent apartment. He took a shower, pulled on jeans and a light sweater. Twilight faded into night outside his windows, and he auto-matically turned on the lights. He turned on his stereo, putting in tapes he didn't listen to. When the doorbell rang, he went to answer it, still moving by rote. Until he opened the door.

"The mountain wouldn't come to Mohammed," she murmured.

She was leaning against the doorjamb gracefully, her slender figure set off by a clinging black dress; it boasted a deep V neckline, a slit almost to her hip revealing one shapely leg, and had long, flowing sleeves. Her glorious hair was piled loosely atop her head. Diamond studs sparkled in her lobes, and a small diamond pendant lay alluringly in the valley between her breasts.

"I came to take you to dinner."

Before he could respond, she gestured slightly, and

Trevor fell back in surprise as three white-jacketed waiters filed past him. Turning slightly, he watched as they set the table by the window with white cloth and candles, silverware, stemware—everything. They produced it all from the baskets they carried, finally unpacking several covered dishes and a bottle of chilled wine. Then, just as silently and efficiently, they filed back out of the apartment.

"Thanks, Eric," Taylor murmured.

The last waiter to leave sent her a quick smile and an "Anytime" in response, then they were gone.

Belatedly remembering his manners, Trevor stepped back and gestured for her to come in. As she moved past him, he caught the elusive scent of a truly devastating perfume. He shut the door and followed her into the living room, clearing his throat determinedly.

"Taylor, you—"

"French food," she interrupted blandly, turning to face him. "It fit my mood."

He stared at her. "Which is?"

She looked wounded. "Can't you tell?"

"Seductive?" he guessed.

"I'm glad you noticed."

Trevor cleared his throat a second time. It was impossible for him to be brusque with her, equally impossible to attempt a serious conversation while she regarded him with that wickedly humorous look in her eyes. So he found himself falling back on the teasing, companionable mood he'd missed these last days.

"You could," he told her definitely, "seduce Mount Rushmore—all four of them—in that dress."

"What works on granite doesn't work on man?"

"This man is putty in your hands," he assured her in a rueful voice. "You came loaded for bear and found a puppy instead."

She giggled. "Then I won't have to strip down to the teddy to get your attention?" she added innocently.

To his throat-clearing, Trevor added swallowing. She'd caught him at a perfect time, while he was hovering between what he wanted and what he knew he couldn't have. He could have strangled her. Except that he wanted her in his arms worse than he'd ever wanted anything in his life.

"You ought to be spanked," he said finally.

She appeared interested. "I've never been spanked."

He caught her elbow firmly and steered her toward the table. "Let's eat."

Chapter Six

As Trevor politely pulled her chair out for her, he said, "Is this dinner part of your—uh—"

"Courtship?" She smiled up at him over one shoulder, vivid eyes gleaming with amusement. "Of course it is. Fine food, candlelight, the sexiest dress I could find in my closet." Her blue eyes became merrily critical as he moved toward his own chair. "You aren't dressed for the part, though—one disadvantage of surprises."

"My dinner jacket is at the cleaners," he apologized gravely.

"I'll forgive you."

"Thank you. What would you have done if I'd been . . . entertaining someone else?" he asked mildly, unfolding his napkin.

"You weren't." She watched him pouring the wine.

"But if I had been?"

"What do you think?"

He handed her a glass. "I think you would have innocently confided the date of our wedding to my guest."

Taylor lifted her glass in a little toast. "I probably would have. Or cried," she added reflectively.

"You're dangerous," he told her with some feeling.

She giggled. "Not really."

"Yes, you are. Any woman with a habit of innocently bringing home strange men is dangerous. Add to that a siren's eyes, a voice that could charm lions, a body that could move Mount Rushmore, a deadly ability to defend yourself, and—and—ESP. Dangerous."

Taylor lifted her fork and smiled very sweetly at him.

"And stop smiling at me!" he ordered, harassed. "I don't even know what I'm eating. What am I eating?"

"You know," she observed, ignoring his question, "for a man who claims to be fighting my—um—snare, you say the nicest things."

Trevor very pointedly ignored this, paying strict attention to his food. But finally his curiosity got the better of him. Half-glaring at her serene face across the table, he muttered, "D'you really have a teddy on under that dress?"

"Black lace," she confirmed gently. "And garters."

He blinked, forgetting to glare. "Garters? Do women still wear those things?"

"They do when they're out to seduce."

"Dammit, Taylor!"

"Just a friendly warning," she explained blandly.

Trevor drained his wineglass and filled it up again. Methodically.

She giggled again. "Well, I did—um—give notice of intent, Trevor. I warned you that I'd chase you."

"Wanton," he managed.

"Thank you," she replied cordially.

He fought manfully against his baser instincts. "Taylor, your father should have locked you in a tower when you were twelve."

"Like Rapunzel?"

"Yes. But your father should have kept your hair short."

"But my prince couldn't have reached me," she objected.

"My point exactly."

"You don't think I deserve a prince?"

"Let's say rather that it would take an extremely *unusual* prince to deserve you."

She thought about that. "I think I've been insulted."

"On the contrary."

Taylor smiled her sweet, mischievous smile and held out her empty glass to him. "Well, I think my prince is unusual enough to cope."

He hesitated before filling her glass. "First tell me how you hold your wine."

"By my thumbs," she confessed sunnily.

Trevor sighed and poured three fingers into the glass. "If I take you home drunk, your father'll kill me."

"I'm of age, darling," she reminded him.

The endearment caught him off guard, and when he met the blue eyes smiling at him across the table, he saw warmth behind the amusement. A steady, inviting, unsettling warmth. A very large part of him wanted nothing more than to cast aside the very real doubts he felt and allow instinct to take over. But he loved her too much to deliberately risk hurting her.

He broke free of her eyes, pushing his chair back and getting to his feet, glass in hand. He stepped down from the raised dining area into the living room and went over to the fireplace, a luxury feature few apartments in the building boasted. Setting the glass on the mantel, he reached for a box of matches. "Late in the year for a fire," he murmured. "But—"

"There's a chill in the air," she said softly.

Trevor made no response to that, bending to kindle the fire, but he was very much aware that she'd left the table. When he straightened from his task and turned, he saw that she had borrowed a couple of pillows from the couch and now sat on the thickly carpeted floor with her back to the love seat flanking the fireplace. One of the pillows was placed invitingly for him.

Retrieving his glass, he joined her with a reluctance born of the knowledge that his determination not to hurt her was no match for both his building desire— and her guileless "seduction." He found himself sitting beside her, one elbow resting on the love seat's cushion as he half turned toward her; her own position matched his, and she lifted her glass in a tiny salute, smiling, before sipping the ruby liquid.

"Taylor . . . we have to talk," he said, trying for

firmness and hearing, without surprise, the rough un-evenness of his voice.

"You want to talk about all your noble scruples," she murmured.

"Stop reading my mind!"

She looked surprised. "I didn't. I read your face."

Trevor got hold of himself. "Whatever. Look, we haven't known each other very long."

"No," she admitted, then spoiled the logic of this by adding simply, "but I feel as if I've known you forever."

He fought against being disarmed. "Still, the fact remains that we're virtual strangers."

"No," she objected, "we aren't strangers. And we have a great deal in common. We both like mysteries and baseball, old movies and animals, chess and jig-saw puzzles. We have the same tastes in music and politics. We both hate snails and peanut butter." She reflected for a moment, frowning. "The only things left to establish, I think, are if you mind taking out the garbage and if you sleep with the window open or closed."

Trevor now had a dual battle on his hands. He was fighting the baser instincts set alight by a combination of love, desire, and her intoxicating perfume, and he was fighting the laughter that her solemn, ridiculous conversation inevitably roused.

He cleared his throat. "Taylor—"

"Do you mind taking out the garbage?"

"No. Taylor—"

"Good. I hate it. Do you sleep with the window open or closed?"

"Which do you?"

"Open."

"I like it closed," he announced, perjuring his soul without hesitation.

"I'll adapt," she countered instantly.

Trevor choked. "Taylor, you—"

"Right or left side of the bed?" she asked briskly.

"I," he told her loftily, "sleep all over the bed."

"Well, I'm not very big. I imagine I could find a corner to curl up on."

"I hog the covers. You'd freeze."

"No. I'd just make sure the covers you were hogging contained me."

By now, Trevor's struggle was severe; he was holding on to control by force and fast-fading determination. "I snore!" he announced in a last-ditch effort to preserve them both from her recklessness.

Taylor patted his arm consolingly. "That's a shame. But I can put cotton in my ears, you know."

Trevor set his glass on the floor, buried his face in the love seat's cushion, and laughed until his stomach hurt. By the time he lifted his head, he felt inexplicably better, but the twinkle in the watching blue eyes sent his inner defenses jangling again.

"A *huge* tower!" he told her definitely. "And you should have been *beaten* every day and twice on Sunday!"

"I need a husband to curb my reckless ways," she told the ceiling soulfully.

"You need a cage!"

"I thought I needed a tower."

"That was before. *Now* you need a cage."

Abruptly, the laughter was gone, and she was gazing at him with huge, grave, honest eyes. "I need you," she whispered.

"Taylor..." he breathed, watching his hands reach for her, setting her glass aside, drawing her closer. "You don't know what you're doing."

She came into his arms with the naturalness of infinite trust, her own arms sliding around his neck. "But I do know what I'm doing," she told him throatily. "I know very well what I'm doing."

However much he mistrusted her certainty, however much his own doubts troubled him, Trevor could no more resist her than he could will himself to stop breathing. There was enough of his own determination left to hold desire rigidly in check, to make his kisses as gentle as they were hungry, but when her lips opened invitingly to his, control was shattered.

The insidious warmth crept over him, through him, and he felt a sense of well-being as strong as his desire. Her small hands threaded through his hair, and her slender body molded itself to his. Her mouth was wine-sweet to his exploring tongue, the golden flesh of her back satin beneath his hands as his fingers found the zipper of her dress and slid it down. The heady perfume she wore seemed to envelop them in a cloud and, joined with the kittenlike sounds she made, drove his desire higher in a spiraling, aching ascent.

She was in his bloodstream, a drug he desperately needed more of to satisfy a terrible craving. Never in his life had he felt such desire, such a simple, savage, boundless need. He wanted to lose himself in her, to become a part of her until there was only a sharing one and not a striving two.

Trevor was unaware of moving, yet realized on some observing level of his perceptions that they were lying together on the thick carpet. They were turned toward each other, so close he could feel her heart pounding in time with his, and he could feel her own need rising to meet his with a strength that denied her delicate body. Guided by instinct and hunger, his fingers blindly drew the dress off her shoulders and down her willing arms, the silky material gliding over her smooth flesh and the flimsy satin-and-lace confection she wore beneath it. Her hips lifted slightly to allow the dress its passage, and it slid down her legs to pool in glimmering folds until it was kicked away by careless feet.

He lifted his head at last, breathing roughly, unevenly, staring down at her slender form. The diamond glittered with her quick breaths; black satin and lace cupped her breasts lovingly and hugged her flat stomach and gently curved hips. The promised garters were frilly, silly things, stark black against her golden skin, and the sheer stockings they guarded turned flesh to silk. Her tiny feet were hosed only, the delicate sandals long since kicked away.

"God, you're so lovely," he said hoarsely, his gaze returning to her beautiful, fascinating face. The vivid eyes were dark with desire, fixed on his face. Her fingers lifted to trace his features gently, and an artless smile curved her lips.

"No one's ever looked at me like that before," she whispered wonderingly.

He kissed her fingers, smothered by his heart's

thundering, aching all over with needing her. Tenderness warred with bemusement as he thought of her assured aplomb in "seducing" him; she could dress in sexy clothes and wear them as if seduction were an art she knew well, yet his own hungry yearning brought wonder to her eyes.

Unusual . . . God, yes, she was unusual!

"Sometimes I think you're twelve years old," he said huskily. "And other times . . . other times you seem older than you have any right to be."

Her arms encircled his neck, and her smile became a very feminine thing. "I'm old enough to know what I want," she murmured.

Vivid blue promises called him, snared him, and Trevor managed only a few words before banked, smoldering fire burst its bounds. "What you want— may not be good for you."

"I'll chance it," she whispered against his lips.

He was dimly aware of a niggling sense of unease, of doubt and uncertainty, but it all seemed far away and unimportant. Until he lifted his head again to see the trust shining in her eyes. Then the faraway stormed up and stared him down, his own conscience battering him.

Abruptly, feeling as if he left a part of himself in her arms, Trevor forced his aching body to obey him. He drew away from her, sat up. Back against the love seat, he stared into the fireplace blindly.

Taylor sat up slowly. She was gazing at him quietly. "Why?"

"Because you're so damned sure—" he burst out, halting when his voice broke raggedly.

Taylor nodded, as if to herself. "Because I'm so sure how it's going to end."

"And I'm not!" He gestured roughly. "Dammit, Taylor, d'you think I don't know you wouldn't make love with a man unless you were certain he'd be the father of your children one day? Of course I know it!"

"Of course," she agreed softly, eyes glowing.

"But *I'm* not sure that man is me," he said, gruff now. "And I won't—take a gift that might well belong to another man."

Taylor was smiling; in fact, she appeared on the verge of giggles. "You mean you won't play a Victorian rake to my Victorian heroine?" she asked unsteadily.

He stared at her for a moment, then choked on a laugh of his own. "God, did I sound that stuffy and noble?" he managed to ask.

She was too busy giggling to reply verbally, but she nodded enthusiastically, and Trevor joined her in laughter when he couldn't hold back any longer.

Taylor got her breath back first. "I'm so glad you found me crying in that park," she told him fervently.

He cleared his throat carefully of the final chuckle. "I haven't made up my mind whether I'm glad or not. But, stuffiness aside, you know what I meant."

"Yes." She smiled at him. "It's very gallant of you, Trevor, not to take advantage of me."

She's done it again, the little witch! Made me laugh when I ought to be feeling something else. God, she looks adorable in that teddy! Ruthlessly, he tore his mind away from how she looked. Or tried to. Whether she knew it or not, only her invariable habit of making him laugh saved her from ravishment. "Stop sounding so damned solemn—you'll set me off again!" he complained.

Plaintively, she went on, "After I *waited* for you all these years, *saved* myself for you, collected a *trousseau* in anticipation—"

"Did you?" he asked, intrigued. "Collect a trousseau?"

"I have my grandmother's handmade quilt and cast iron skillet," she said solemnly.

Trevor choked. "What—no wedding gown?"

"Mother's," she said serenely.

He carefully grasped sobriety and held on tight. "Enough of this. We have to be serious. This is a serious situation, Taylor."

"Agreed." She was frowning gravely at him now. "And I'm much appreciative of your understanding the seriousness of this situation."

He put his head in his hands.

"After all," she went on loftily, "we're adults. And this is the Age of Aquarius. Or maybe that was before. Anyway, we're certainly capable of resolving this very serious situation. We only have to be reasonable and logical about it." She blinked at him as he raised his head, adding severely, "Except that I don't want to be reasonable and logical. Let's be unreasonable and illogical. Let's make love."

Trevor pulled on a stern face. "You're a forward wench!"

"And you're a backward suitor!"

"Is that what I am?" he wondered, amazed.

"Yes!" She kept her mouth firm, but her eyes danced irrepressibly. "I went to a great deal of trouble to seduce you tonight, and you had to let your scruples rear their ugly heads. I'd planned on being a fallen woman by midnight!"

"You look like one now," he managed unsteadily. "Curled up like a cat on my carpet wearing nothing but that ridiculous bit of black lace. And garters. *Garters*. And not even the decency to ask for your dress!"

"Decency," she said austerely, "can go by the board. Besides, I asked Mother for advice, and *she* suggested the black lace and garters."

Trevor's mind boggled. "You asked your mother—"

"How to seduce you. Well, not that exactly, but what to wear. She said she caught Daddy with black lace and garters."

Searching in vain for words to express himself, Trevor finally uttered an elusive sound somewhere between a strangled laugh and a bear's growl.

"Something caught in your throat?" she inquired innocently, eyes limpid.

He picked up his discarded wineglass, drained it very scientifically, and, now better able to deal with madness, cleared his throat. "Do you mean to tell me that you told your mother you were going to seduce me?"

"I knew she'd be interested," she explained gravely.

"Oh," he responded carefully. "You knew she'd be interested."

"Certainly. And Daddy said—"

"Him, too," Trevor told the ceiling in a faint voice that suggested his cup was more than full.

Taylor ignored the interruption. "—that there was just something *about* black lace and garters. The male libido, I suppose."

"Do you?" He eyed her in utter fascination. "And that's all your loving parents had to say about the matter?"

"Well, when Mother suggested the teddy, Daddy said they were the very devil to get off—"

Trevor choked.

"—but Mother reminded him that Christmas presents wouldn't be half the fun to open if they weren't wrapped up in shiny paper. And after he thought about it, he agreed with her."

"I'll bet," Trevor said weakly.

"So then Mother gave me this necklace; she said it was meant to be a coming-of-age present, and to-night looked like as good a time as any. And Daddy told me to kick my shoes off at the proper moment, because they could get confoundedly in the way." Taylor looked thoughtful. "And since Mother started laughing when he said that, I imagine he spoke from experience, don't you?"

Trevor was laughing too hard to answer. He could picture that scene so vividly in his mind, seeing Sara's vague smile and Luke's absently paternal expression, both of them uttering their wonderfully unconventional, ridiculous, *absurd* advice in the most matter-of-fact way. In that moment, he would have traded his bank account for the privilege of having been present to see and hear them advise their firstborn in the art of seduction.

"And *now*," Taylor said sadly, "after they went to all that trouble, and I tried so hard to be sexy, *you* had to ruin everything with your silly scruples."

"Sorry!" he gasped.

"You should be! I've waited twenty-six years for you, buster—"

"Consoled by occasional strange foreign and domestic men," he pointed out meaningfully.

"That's beside the point. I was waiting for you to come along—and very patient I've been, too! There I was expecting a macho prince to come along and carry me off over his saddle, and instead I get Sir Walter Raleigh spreading his cloak over a puddle so I won't get my feet wet!"

Trevor went off again.

With no mercy, Taylor continued in the same fiercely put-upon voice. "I wanted more Don Juan—less Sir Galahad! I wanted the Black Knight instead of the White Knight! I wanted to be ravished totally—well, partially—against my will! I wanted a dash of James Bond and a pinch of Superman and a slice or two of the Lone Ranger—"

"A macho salad!" Trevor laughed even harder at the affronted expression she wore; it was belied by the wicked laughter in her eyes.

"And if we're going to talk about *decency*," she said roundly with only a faint quiver to betray her, "why don't we talk about a man who won't even let himself be decently seduced!"

"That's a contradiction in terms," he said a bit weakly.

"Not," she said, "in my dictionary, it isn't."

Trevor wiped his streaming eyes and tried to gather some vague sort of command over himself. He felt completely limp with laughter, utterly relaxed, and wholly incapable of logical thought.

"Feeling better?" she murmured suddenly.

Trevor stared at her. "You've been manipulating me, you little witch," he realized slowly.

"You were upset." Her lovely face was ingenuous. "And they do say laughter's the best medicine, after all."

He had a feeling his mouth was open and hastily closed it. He knew better than to doubt anything she'd said—particularly about her parents—but he realized his love had been playing him like a piano tuned expertly to her touch. "Three hundred years ago," he said ruefully, "you'd have been burned at the stake."

Her eyes gleamed at him. "Probably. But admit it—you do feel better."

Trevor sighed. "Yes, I feel better. I'm still not sure I'm the man for you, however."

"You laugh at my jokes," she pointed out. "And that's a more solid basis for marriage than most people ever find."

Just as she'd very nearly seduced him with black lace and garters, she now came close to performing the feat a second time. A part of him longed wistfully to share his life with a woman who could make him laugh—and feel better—in spite of himself. But there was still that part of him wary of being *too* well known.

She could read his mind.

Accordingly, he shied off again. "I'll grant that," he said carefully, "but I'm still not sure. And bear in mind, young lady, that I'll not be seduced against my will!"

"Funny, for a while there, I thought you were willing."

Trevor sent a mock glare toward her gently quizzical expression. "You know damn well I was, and stop baiting me!"

"Sorry," she murmured, still smiling.

"And now," he said sternly, "if you'll get de——uh—dressed, I'll take you home."

"I can't go home tonight," she objected.

He eyed her with foreboding. "Why not?"

"Because I'm supposed to be seducing you," she explained patiently. "If I come home before dawn, Mother and Daddy'll know I failed. Their very own daughter a failure as a temptress! Just imagine—they won't be able to hold their heads up again at their club!"

"Do they have a club?" he asked involuntarily.

"Of course they have a club, Trevor."

He got hold of himself again. "Well, no one else has to know, so they can hold their heads up."

"Trevor," she said in a very gentle, long-suffering voice, "you know my parents. D'you really believe no one else will know?"

He thought about it for a moment, then matched her tone of long-suffering. "I suppose they *would* consider it dinner-table conversation at that."

"Tennis-court conversation at the very least. And

even if *they* can hold their heads up, *I'll* be utterly shamed! You wouldn't do that to me, would you?"

Trevor sighed, defeated. "If you'll promise me I won't face a shotgun wedding in the morning—"

"Trevor!"

"That," he said roundly, "is no promise!"

She giggled. "I promise. No shotgun wedding."

"I'm too limp to argue," he confessed wryly.

"Good. Listen, there's a dandy old movie on the late show tonight. D'you think—?"

"Why not?" He sighed again, then said in a stronger voice, "Now, since you're obviously too shameless to put your dress back on, I'm going to go find you a robe."

Taylor looked down at herself in some surprise. "I'd forgotten."

"I hadn't!" he said definitely, and he went in search of a robe with which to cover his love's distracting charms.

Chapter Seven

IT DIDN'T TAKE long to clear up the remains of Taylor's candlelight dinner. Items borrowed from her restaurant friend were washed and packed neatly back into their baskets so they could be returned the next day.

Then it was time for the late show.

A bowl of popcorn sat decorously between them on the couch. Taylor, who had categorically refused to don her dress on the grounds that what was comfortable for seduction was uncomfortable for television-viewing, was nearly swallowed whole by Trevor's blue velour robe. Legs crossed at the ankles and feet propped on his coffee table, she chatted amiably to him during commercials, clearly undisturbed by her failure to seduce him.

The violent emotions and laughter of the evening had taken their toll on Trevor. He divided his bemused attention between the TV screen and Taylor's profile, trying mentally to light a fire under those scruples of his so that he could insist on taking her home. But that fire would only sputter and die.

She'd forced his hand by coming to him, but he couldn't find it in himself to be sorry about that. Fighting his own desire to be with her had turned him into a restless, angry bear for five interminable days. He loved being with her. She turned his world upside down, but she made him laugh, and a dim part of him recognized that he hadn't laughed enough in his life.

No matter how determined he was to edge himself painlessly out of her life, he knew ruefully just how useless that determination was; if he'd had to fight only himself or only her he might have managed to walk away from her. He couldn't fight them both. And whenever he allowed himself to hope he might be able to live with her unusual gifts, a dark and primitive panic stirred in his mind.

It certainly occurred to him that he'd felt no discomfort in being with Taylor since that first day, but he couldn't deceive himself into believing the battle won. It might not have bothered him too much thus far, but there was a vast difference between a couple of weeks and thirty or forty years. And he knew himself too well not to be certain that he needed the privacy of his own mind.

Now, as they watched an old horror movie on television, he silently acknowledged the fact that he needed her, too. It was more than love, or at least more than he knew love to be. He was not fanciful, but he thought that the "more than love" he felt might well be an instinctive recognition of—a kindred spirit. More, perhaps. The other half of himself . . . perhaps.

Could he, with the best of intentions, with the best will in the world, walk away from that?

"You're getting upset again," she said softly.

"Stop reading my mind."

Her vivid, honest eyes gazed at him quizzically. "I don't have to read your mind; your face is grim."

"I'm a lousy companion, in fact," he said lightly.

"No. Just a troubled one. Are you . . . angry with me, Trevor?"

He blinked in surprise. "With you? No, of course not. Why should I be angry with you?"

Taylor's smile was a little crooked. "Well, I haven't exactly been conventional. In fact, as you said, I've been shameless. But have I been . . . wrong?"

"Wrong?" He bit back a sudden laugh. "Taylor, that's a hell of a question to ask me."

"Why?"

"Because I don't know right from wrong when I'm with you." Then he corrected himself wryly. "No, that isn't true. I know what's wrong, and it isn't you. It's me."

"Wrong for me, you mean?"

He nodded silently.

"But, why?" She half turned on the couch, folding her legs and resting an arm on the low back of the couch as she gazed seriously at him.

Her candid eyes drew the truth from him even though he was afraid it might well hurt her. "Because

I'm—not comfortable with telepathy." He saw a tiny frown form in her eyes and tried to think of some way to make the truth less hurtful. "I've always believed there should be honesty in any relationship, but it's—unnerving to know I might as well speak every thought out loud. I catch myself putting up walls I shouldn't need, being guarded when I don't want to be. It isn't *you,* Taylor. It's me."

She reached for the remote control and turned the television off, then dropped it back on the coffee table and faced him again, and her expression was distressed. "Oh, Trevor, I'm sorry! I should have explained."

"Explained what?" He was gruff, feeling that he'd kicked something small and loving.

Taylor took a deep breath, clearly gathering her thoughts. "What being telepathic really means. I guess I didn't explain before now because it—it isn't *easy* to explain."

"You don't have to—"

"Yes." She gazed at him steadily. "I have to." A sudden and rueful twinkle lit her eyes. "You're perfectly entitled to sacrifice yourself on the altar of useless scruples, but I'll be damned if I'll let you sacrifice me!"

"What?" he managed, wondering when he'd lost the thread of the conversation.

"Well, maybe the choice of words was wrong, but you're putting up walls needlessly, Trevor. And if *that's* all that's standing between us, then I have to make you understand."

He nodded. "All right. But I don't see—"

"And neither do I," she interrupted firmly. "If you're afraid I'm constantly seeing into your mind, you're wrong. I've been telepathic all my life, and after twenty-six years I've learned to build walls—necessary walls—of my own. If I didn't, I'd go crazy."

"Because of the . . . mental chatter?" he asked.

"Yes. It'd be like standing in a huge room with people talking all around me; nothing would make sense, but it'd be *loud*. When I meet someone for the first time, a kind of door opens in my mind very briefly. Partly, I think, because telepathy is just another sense, and it's an old instinct to use all the senses in weighing up a stranger. But for me to deliberately open that door and look into someone's mind unnecessarily would be a horrible intrusion."

Trevor tried in vain to find the words to express the dark stirrings of panic he still felt. "But—you *can* read minds."

She seemed to realize what he meant. "Yes, but only the topmost level of consciousness. For instance, when we met, you were thinking of your brother, your job, and a restaurant you'd had dinner at the night before. Impressions from all of those were tangled in your thoughts; all I received was a *sense* of you made up of those impressions. No matter how hard I tried, I could never pull a complete thought out of your mind—just an impression of what you were thinking."

Taylor shook her head slightly. "If I'd worked all my life to sharpen that sense, maybe I could read coherent thoughts. But I can't. I can only see a tiny part of a very *surface* part of another mind. The majority of that mind is as hidden from me as it is from anyone with no ESP."

"You found that killer," he said, remembering the newspaper articles he'd read days before.

She paled slightly, her eyes going briefly dark. "The mind of a killer," she said in a low voice, "is very different from a normal mind. It . . . shouts. It isn't hard to focus on that kind of mind, but I still get only impressions."

Regretting his unthinking remark, Trevor attempted to draw her thoughts away from that dark mind she'd seen. "You always seem to know what I'm thinking," he said with forced lightness.

"Not what you're *thinking*," she corrected. "What you're *feeling*. I mean, I always know your—your mood. That isn't telepathy, Trevor. It's empathy."

More than a little startled, Trevor realized then that he was usually very aware of *her* moods. Empathy? Recognition of a kindred spirit? He put the thought aside and focused on one of the most insidious, pleasant, unnerving facets of her telepathy. "Whenever we touch," he said slowly, "I feel a strong sense of—of well-being. As if I were wrapped in a blanket."

"You, too?" Her honest eyes held a shy, delighted smile. "I thought it was just me."

"It has nothing to do with your telepathy?" he asked incredulously, all his doubts and preconceptions swaying on their foundations.

"I've never felt that before, so I don't think so." She leaned toward him anxiously. "Trevor, I haven't read your mind since that first day."

"You haven't?"

"No."

Impossible to doubt those naked eyes. He felt a heavy load lift from his shoulders. "Well, hell, why didn't you tell me?" he demanded wrathfully.

She laughed unsteadily. "How was I to know? Since I didn't read your mind, I just assumed you were bothered by my chasing you!"

Surprised yet again, Trevor said blankly, "I suppose I should have been, but, you know, that never bothered me at all."

"And you called *me* shameless! Being chased pandered to your ego, didn't it? Admit it!"

He grinned. "Well, I've never gotten flowers or candy before. It was a . . . novel experience."

Taylor lifted the bowl of popcorn between them, looking at him with a solemn expression and dancing eyes. "Do we really need this duenna anymore?"

He could hardly help but laugh. "No. *If* you've given up your intention of seducing me tonight. I still think we need a little time. Without walls between us now."

"If you insist. But I already know everything I need to know." She leaned over to place the bowl on the coffee table, then used the remote control to turn the television back on.

Trevor slipped an arm around her as she curled up at his side. "Oh, you do, do you?"

"Certainly. I know that you're a humorous, caring, sensitive man. I really don't need to know anything else."

"I thought you said I wasn't macho enough," he objected dryly.

"Only where your scruples and my virtue are concerned. Otherwise, you're perfect."

"I'll try to do better next time, ma'am," he murmured, humble.

Blue eyes glinted up at him before returning to the television screen. "I'll make certain of it," she said gently.

The late show turned out to be an all-night horror festival, and somewhere in the middle of it they both fell asleep. It was an easy thing to accomplish, since they'd stretched out during the second movie by mutual consent, both turned facing the set with Taylor's back to Trevor and his arms around her.

Trevor had never slept so well. He woke to bright sunlight streaming through the windows, hearing the murmur of an early news program on television and feeling the warmth of her in his arms.

It was, he decided, a very nice way to wake up.

"You *don't* snore," she murmured.

"That's odd. I thought I did."

"Liar."

"So I told one small white lie. *You* came here with the fixed intention of seducing me."

"I'm shameless, and you're a liar. Don't we make a perfect couple?"

"I plead the fifth amendment."

"Coward."

He laughed softly, tightening his arms around her. "I won't bother trying to defend myself on that one. Instead, why don't we have breakfast?"

"Does it occur to you that we spend a great deal

of our time together either cooking or eating?"

"It crossed my mind. D'you suppose there's some Freudian meaning behind that?"

"Likely just hunger," she said practically. She sat up and swung her feet to the floor as he released her, looking down at him with a smile.

He gazed up at her for a moment, taking in the tousled chestnut hair and bright blue eyes. The robe's belt had worked loose during the night, the open lapels revealing black silk and lace; Trevor silently acquitted her of deliberate enticement, but he had to swallow hard before he could speak. "I might have known," he muttered in a long-suffering tone, "you'd look as beautiful in the morning as you do any other time."

Taylor leaned down and kissed him fleetingly, her hand lingering on his cheek. "Thank you, sir," she said gravely. "You look pretty good yourself—in spite of the stubble."

For the first time in his adult life, Trevor found a distinct pleasure in his fairly heavy morning beard; the tingling caress of her fingers was one for which he would have willingly let his razor grow rusty. "I have to shave," he said reluctantly.

"Only if you want to," she said. "I don't object to beards."

Dryly, he asked, "Is there anything you do object to?"

"Yes. Eggs in the morning." She stood up, absently drawing the robe's lapels together and tightening the belt. She stretched slightly, unconsciously luxuriating in the blissful morning action. "Do you like waffles?"

"Love 'em."

"Then if you have the fixings, that's what I'll make."

He got to his feet, stretching as unconsciously as she had. "I have the fixings, but you shouldn't have to cook; you're a guest."

"Forced on you against your will," she recalled soulfully. "Cooking will be my penance."

Trevor managed to swat her once on the fanny before she escaped, laughing, to the kitchen. He smiled after her for a moment, realized abruptly that he probably looked like a besotted teenager, then mentally decided not to give a damn. Feeling much more cheerful today than he had yesterday morning, he went off to shave.

He'd once heard a woman say that shaving to a man was like washing dishes to a woman—before electric dishwashers; it was an automatic, curiously soothing action, allowing the mind to range free. Trevor agreed that shaving tended to free the mind; he'd more than once worked out some tricky problem or legal question while gazing absently into a steamed mirror.

This morning, his mind focused inevitably on Taylor and their night together. The evening before was divided by his mind into four separate and distinct parts. Part one had been seduction, part two had been laughter, part three revelation, and part four an amazingly restful sleep. For the first two, he felt no surprise; seduction and laughter were quite definitely a part of their relationship. The fourth part amazed him only because he wasn't a gibbering idiot after holding her platonically in his arms all night.

Part three occupied his thoughts. Revelation. He never hesitated in accepting her assurances regarding the telepathy. She didn't read his mind, and that meant that there was no reason for the wall he'd built between them. However, he knew the wall still existed in a ghostly form, elusive and still vaguely troubling.

And he couldn't fully commit himself until he was certain that faint barrier posed no threat to them.

He pondered that wall as he shaved. It was formed of fear, he thought, a primitive and unreasoning fear of the unknown and the misunderstood. Applying logic in a determined attempt to breach that fear, he reminded himself that there was only a tiny part of his mind she could see into *anyway*. It helped, but the wall remained a nebulous threat.

Trevor thought he could deal with it eventually. Experience. A surer knowledge of Taylor gained through time. A gradual relaxing of the guards people inevitably raised against one another in the tentative beginnings of a relationship.

Wanting that relationship, he thought, would go a long way in helping. And he very badly wanted Taylor to become a permanent part of his life. She made him feel a better man than he knew himself to be, a fact he acknowledged with an inner rueful sigh. There were no rosy glasses blinding Taylor's honest eyes; she knew well that he was far from perfect. But she thought him perfect for her, and for that very unusual and fascinating woman to believe that of him was a compliment Trevor found both moving and bemusing.

Belonging to Taylor.

It meant laughing. And loving. It meant being known and understood, a fact that caused a faint uneasy quiver to disturb some deep part of him, but was, on some other level of himself, curiously pleasing.

But . . . could he ever know her that well? She was endlessly fascinating, his love, blessed with the gifts of humor and tolerance and honesty. Her unconventional upbringing had left her with few subtleties or feminine evasions at her command; she would never be blunt to the point of hurting another, but she'd always be honest, he knew.

Abruptly, superimposed over his own cloudy image in the mirror, he saw those honest eyes staring at him blindly.

"I wish it was the other way around. I wish I could cry when it mattered and not when it didn't."

A sensitive woman, her vulnerability for the most part hidden within her—like those unshed tears that mattered. A woman who was the calm, practical hub around which her ridiculous family turned, and yet who could herself become absurd at the drop of a hat. She was invariably cheerful, yet her psychic gift had shown her the darker side of humanity, had given her eyes to see into a madman's sick, murderous thoughts.

And not just one madman, Trevor realized painfully; she felt "a responsibility to do what I can to help." To help capture madmen, she'd willingly expose herself to those dark and twisted thoughts.

Automatically wiping away the steam obscuring the mirror, Trevor gazed into his own suddenly blind eyes.

She believed he was the man for her, and he realized then that he had never really considered their relationship from her point of view. "Sensitive," she'd called him. *Fool!* he called himself. He knew that he'd nearly had it once, nearly realized why she needed him—and it had thrown him into a blind panic.

She didn't need the dark gremlins hidden in his own mind; she only needed his willingness to share them.

That was all. All! If he could be willing to share his vulnerability, then she would share hers. It would not be an exchange of dark and guilty secrets, hurts, fears, but a simple knowing and understanding of them. Trust. Openness. And most of all . . . love.

Trevor had heard all the rhetoric. Times had changed. *People* had changed. Women could be strong and men sensitive. Women could be assertive and men understanding. Women could be forceful and men intuitive. But knowing it *could* be done was only half the problem solved.

Knowing that a man could cry made his unshed tears no easier than those a strong woman held at bay within her.

Taylor couldn't cry when it mattered, and neither could Trevor.

For her, he thought, the tears refused to come because her psychic abilities guarded her mind so carefully. For him, he knew, the tears a boy might have learned to shed had been deeply buried by a man's responsibilities. He'd been eighteen when their parents had been killed, his own shock and grief numbed by the necessity of raising his ten-year-old brother.

Jason had been able to cry, but Trevor, willingly accepting the role of parent, had buried his own tears, comforted Jason as best he could, and picked up the threads of their lives. And his brother would never know, although he might well guess, the sleepless nights and anxiety that had tormented Trevor. Their parents had left them far from penniless, but Trevor had struggled nonetheless in raising Jason and putting them both through school.

He regretted none of it, but he wished now that he'd allowed himself to share his brother's tears. For, having once accepted a stoic path, Trevor had found it impossible to retrace his steps. How could he be vulnerable when Jason had needed him to be strong?

How indeed.

But Jason had his own life now. And Trevor could see now how that first stoic step had molded his way of thinking. Even his choice of law as a career had reinforced the impassive surface of himself. How many times had he swayed a jury with emotional rhetoric while a part of him had watched analytically for the reaction he sought?

He'd learned to play with the emotions of others while keeping his own tightly bound in dark silence. Even his love for Jason had been an unspoken thing, proving itself in gruff gestures rather than words. Thankfully, Jason had seen through to the truth, Trevor thought.

And Taylor . . . Taylor. She called it empathy, this sensing of moods and understanding of them. She with the naked eyes holding the power to pull emotions from him and tease him into enjoying it. She had brought his emotions much closer to the surface — because *she* needed that as much as he did.

The other half of himself . . . the emotional, intuitive part of him buried for so long. They were, he realized with a sudden flash of insight, almost mirror images of each other—but reversed. His mind flew back to that first day. Taylor, on the surface a cheerful woman brought easily to laughter or tears, but underneath so very controlled because she'd been forced to build shields around her sensitive mind and heart. Trevor, outwardly controlled and stoic, calm and logical, but inwardly a caldron boiling with nearly fifteen years of suppressed love, laughter, and tears.

In a blink of time, Taylor had begun guilelessly to free those tightly bound emotions within him. And laughter, because it comes easiest, had fought its way free first. Love was struggling, but the chains binding it were snapping one by one. Tears would be the most difficult to free.

And Taylor, he realized slowly, had begun changing herself. There was now a curious blending of the very cheerful woman and the controlled one. Absurd as her humor sometimes was, there were deeper meanings to it now—such as when she had deliberately roused him to laughter to ease his troubled mind. And she had allowed him to glimpse the vulnerable part of her, to see her pain at a madman's thoughts, to see her diffidence at her own reckless "seduction" plans. The wonder at seeing herself reflected in a man's— his—passionate eyes.

Trevor grappled with the thoughts as he left the bathroom and headed for the kitchen. They could free each other, he realized dimly. Somehow, through an elusive but very real . . . empathy . . . they could free each other from cages only vaguely perceived.

He stopped in the doorway of the kitchen and

watched her silently. She looked tiny and fragile in his robe, the sleeves turned back several times on her slender arms and the hem falling past her knees. Her hair was still gloriously tousled, the pins that had confined it last night now lost and unremembered. She was handling the waffle iron with the expert touch of a born cook and humming softly to herself.

He banked his thoughts carefully in his mind and stepped into the room. Whether those thoughts were right or wrong would only be proven, he knew, with time.

She looked over her shoulder at him, smiling. "I was afraid you'd cut your throat," she confided, neatly flipping the golden-brown waffles onto plates.

"Nope. Didn't even nick myself." It didn't surprise him to hear his own calm, bantering tone; with Taylor, falling into a companionable mood was rather like one foot automatically following the other.

They sat down at the breakfast table in the kitchen, and for a while conversation was limited to the mundane but necessary.

"Would you pass the butter, please?"

"Certainly. More coffee?"

"Thank you."

With the meal nearly finished, Trevor said, "Are you sure there'll be no shotgun wedding on the agenda?"

"I promised, didn't I?" she countered serenely.

He looked at her. "Under these circumstances with any other family, I'd be tempted to ask why not. With your family, I'm afraid to hear the answer."

Taylor's eyes were filled with mischief. "Well, I'm

not saying that Daddy wouldn't rouse himself enough to defend his daughter's honor, you understand."

"Then why no shotgun wedding?" His gaze narrowed suspiciously. "If your father decks me the way he did the Frenchman—"

She laughed. "No, of course he won't. Trevor, you forget—my entire family's psychic. Daddy'll know the instant he sees me that my virtue is still very much intact."

Trevor blinked. Then, dryly, he said, "I *did* forget, dammit. You little witch. So they'll never be able to hold their heads up at the club, huh?"

After sipping her coffee, Taylor smiled seraphically. "I was worried about the *neighbors* seeing me."

"You were not. We agreed—I remember distinctly—that your parents couldn't resist telling everyone that you weren't, in spite of all efforts, a fallen woman. You were determined to spend the night here, weren't you? No, never mind answering that. It's obvious. Just tell me why." Trevor was looking forward to one of her ridiculous answers, and he wasn't disappointed.

"Well," she said seriously, "I was rather hoping to be ravished in the middle of the night. But you slept like the dead."

"Sorry," he managed faintly, fighting the desire to burst out laughing.

"You should be!" she scolded. "I even managed to get us both in a prone position on the couch—and you fell asleep. Asleep!" Frowning slightly, she asked quizzically, "Should I try a different perfume? Or maybe a lavender teddy instead of black?"

Trevor fought manfully. "Has it occurred to you that it wasn't a question of your—uh—seductiveness, but rather my willpower?"

"Was that it?" she asked, interested. "I didn't do anything wrong?"

"Nothing that I noticed," he said ruefully.

"We," she said firmly, "have to talk further about these noble scruples of yours."

"We've already talked about them. We're going to take the time to get to know each other—remember?"

"But I'm not getting any younger," she protested, aggrieved. "And I want babies!"

He eyed her, fascinated. "What'll you say next?"

"Whatever pops into my head." She grinned suddenly, the vivid blue eyes wickedly amused.

Trevor drew a deep breath and pushed his chair back. "I'm going to clean up in here, and you're going to get dressed—"

"You do want babies, don't you?" she interrupted briskly.

"A hint toward the stability of our future relationship," he advised in a careful tone. "Never—never—ask me loaded questions before nine A.M."

"All right," she said agreeably. "I'll ask again later."

"Much later."

"How much later?"

"Taylor, if you don't go and put your dress on right now—" He broke off and stared into the eyes watching him hopefully. "Witch!" he said feelingly. "Go get dressed!"

Laughing, she slipped from her chair and left the room.

Trevor found himself smiling like a smitten school-boy again and shook his head at himself. A beautiful, seductive woman in his apartment wearing nothing but his robe and a black teddy, and he was ordering her to get dressed.

Ridiculous.

He was obviously losing his mind.

Jason would've split his sides laughing.

Chapter Eight

TREVOR'S WILLPOWER WITHSTOOD the test of zipping Taylor's dress for her, but his finger-and-toehold at the edge of sobriety crumbled—as usual—the moment they entered her house.

With any other family, under the circumstances, Trevor would have accompanied her inside to explain her innocent all-night stay at his apartment; she was over twenty-one, but she lived at home and could have been expected, to some extent, to answer to her father.

However, this was the Shannon family. Trevor didn't go in with her to explain anything at all. He went because he wanted to be with her. And he went because he was curious to see the family's reaction.

Sara entered the hall from the den just as they came

in the front door, and stood gazing at them with her vague gray eyes. Those seemingly hazy eyes took in Taylor's slightly rumpled appearance and blatantly innocent face, then shifted to Trevor's carefully grave face.

"Oh, dear," Sara said mildly but with distressed undertones. "Darling, you can't let it bother you. I'm sure you'll do better next time."

"I plan to, Mother," Taylor responded solemnly.

Trevor bit down hard on his inner cheek in an attempt to fight the laughter.

Sara peered at him, a little doubtful. "You mustn't think I'm being critical, Trevor," she said gently, "but I really think you shouldn't have disappointed the child. She was so looking forward to it."

He choked swallowing the laugh in his throat. He knew only too well that none of his rational arguments would have any effect on Sara, so he didn't attempt any. Holding his voice level with a tremendous effort, he said, "You are an unnatural mother, Sara."

"Am I?" She smiled at him. "I suppose so. But such fun for the children."

Luke wandered in just then, holding a distributor cap. He addressed his wife sternly. "What is this doing in the kitchen?"

"It fell out of the car," she told him.

"They don't just fall out," he objected.

"It did."

Her husband ran a hand through his blond hair, his abstracted expression holding the rueful acceptance of odd things occurring in his wife's orbit. "Well. I'll put it back later."

"The car runs without it," she observed.

He stared at her. "It isn't supposed to."

"It does."

Luke sighed. "It would for you. Not for anyone else. Hello," he added, apparently just noticing his daughter and Trevor. Before they could respond, his brilliant blue eyes became stern again. They focused on Taylor.

"Sorry, Daddy," she said meekly.

The frowning eyes lifted to Trevor, and he fought an instinctive urge to apologize as well. Instead, he met the gaze with all the severity he could muster in his own eyes.

Luke turned back to his wife. "We'll never be able to hold our heads up at the club," he said in a pained voice.

Trevor didn't dare meet Taylor's eyes.

"I know," Sara said seriously. "But I think it was more a matter of Trevor's willpower than Taylor's sex appeal."

Frowning at Trevor, Luke demanded, "Well?"

"Quite true," he answered faintly.

"Willpower," Luke told him in a ridiculously paternal voice, "is a very good thing—in its proper place. But you want to make sure you don't end up being stuffy."

Trevor nodded, not trusting his voice.

"Well, that's all right, then." Luke was cheerful again. "Can you drive a nail? I have to build a tree house for Dory."

"I can drive a nail."

"Then you can help me. Taylor, why don't we barbecue for lunch?"

"All right, Daddy." She sent Trevor a look brimful

of laughter. "I'll go change and then see what we have to barbecue."

"Yes, do," he said absently, already taking Trevor's arm and leading him from the hall.

Trevor went.

The remainder of the morning and early afternoon flew by. Trevor managed not to bruise a thumb or nail his fingers to the tree while assisting Luke to build a tree house. They had barbecued chicken for lunch and a general family clean-up in the kitchen—which meant that it took twice as long to get everything put away neatly with the vaguely incapable "help" of certain members of the family.

Luke instigated a Frisbee game in the backyard and exhausted everyone but himself. They ended up sprawled in various positions beneath the trees, enjoying the shade and quiet as they watched the eldest Shannon industriously weeding a small flower bed in the shade.

Trevor shared the hammock with Taylor, drowsy and content. A part of him was a bit bemused, since she'd several times absently called him "darling." He looked around at the other peaceful members of the family—and one busy one—feeling very much a part of them. Dory was asleep with her head in Sara's lap, Jamie was stretched out nearby on her stomach with a book propped before her, and Jessie leaned against a tree with sheet music in her lap and her fingers playing an imaginary piano.

The blow, when it came, was as out of place in the peaceful scene as such blows always tended to be.

"Trevor."

He turned his head to respond to Luke's voice. Then slowly, he sat up in the hammock, feeling an inexplicable chill. He could feel Taylor's sudden tension as she, too, sat up, both of them staring at her father.

Luke was sitting back on his heels, garden tools overflowing the basket beside him. The tools and the flowers were forgotten. Luke was gazing at Trevor steadily, his brilliant eyes not the least abstracted and his handsome face unusually grim. His voice, when he spoke, held the same curiously chilling evenness that had caught their tense attention.

"Your brother's . . . hiking somewhere."

"In Wyoming."

Taylor softly asked the question Trevor couldn't ask. "What's wrong, Daddy?"

Her father continued to stare intently at Trevor—but through him somehow. As if he were seeing something else entirely. "Have you talked to him?" he asked slowly.

"Not since I put him on the plane Monday." Coldness was seeping all through Trevor, gripping his heart in sudden dread.

Very quietly, Luke said, "Maybe you'd better try getting in touch with him. There'll be a freak blizzard there tomorrow . . . and I think he's in trouble."

Trevor was hardly aware of slipping from the hammock and didn't realize until he was inside the house that he was tightly holding Taylor's hand. The warmth of her hand was the only warmth he felt; all else was coldness. He told himself fiercely that Jason was all right, that he was, even now, staying with his college friend in Casper as he'd planned to do the last few days of his vacation.

He told himself that, but the coldness held him.

It was difficult to think clearly, but Trevor forced himself to. He released Taylor's hand as they reached the telephone in the hall, silently grateful that she remained nearby. He met her anxious eyes, his own a little blind as he grappled mentally for the phone number only dimly remembered from other vacations. Desperation found the number, and steady fingers dialed. He kept his voice calm somehow when a worried voice answered far away.

"Hello?"

"Owen, this is Trevor. Is Jason—"

"Trevor! I've been trying to reach you since this morning."

"What's wrong?" Trevor asked steadily.

Owen sighed raggedly. "Jason was supposed to be back here in Casper yesterday morning. When he never showed, I got worried and called that lodge up in the mountains where he's staying. They sent out a search-and-rescue team, and they've alerted the Rangers. Trevor, there's snow on some of those high peaks, and a blizzard forecast for tomorrow. Jason must have gotten off the trails, or they would have found him by now. And with a storm coming—"

"I'll catch the first flight," Trevor said numbly.

"I'll meet you at the airport."

Trevor cradled the receiver slowly. He stared at Taylor, unable to force a single word past his blocked throat. But out of the fear gripping him rose a sudden terrible need to have her with him. He wasn't thinking of her psychic abilities, but only of her quiet strength. For the first time in his adult life, he needed a strength he couldn't find in himself.

Taylor stepped forward, her hand a comforting touch on his arm. "I may be able to help."

He nodded silently, then reached for the phone again as she hurried upstairs to pack. A toneless voice came from somewhere to book two seats on the next available flight to Casper, and he had to restrain driving impatience when he found that the flight left in two hours. By the time he hung up the phone, Taylor was back with a quilted jacket flung over one arm and a small bag in her other hand.

It was she who quickly and briefly explained the trip to her parents, both of whom were concerned and neither surprised. Luke said only, "He's alive, Trevor." It helped—but not much.

They were quiet on the drive to Trevor's apartment, where he hastily packed a few things. Quiet all the way to the airport and during the interminable wait for their flight.

Trevor paced while he could, then sat beside Taylor on the plane and railed silently at the time it was taking him to get to Jason. He hated the helplessness of not being able to do a damn thing to help his brother, gnawing anxiety tormenting him. And guilt.

Taylor's hand slipped into his as the plane finally took off, and when his fingers closed over hers fiercely, she spoke in a soft voice. "He'll be all right, Trevor."

He stared blindly down at their clasped hands. "I keep telling myself that," he said hoarsely. "I have to believe it. It's just been the two of us for so long..."

"You raised him, didn't you?" Her voice was still soft, gentle. "Tell me about it."

He found himself talking, rapidly and disjointedly. Telling her things he'd not told a living soul until now. About Jason and about himself. About Little League games and parent-teacher meetings, broken arms and bloody noses. About the little anxieties of report cards and neat bedrooms, and the larger ones of late dates and accidents. About his own feelings of ineptitude in assuming the role of parent, his worry at the responsibility for another life. The sleepless nights and careful, anxious balancing of checkbooks.

He told her about teaching Jason to shave, to drive, to cook. About fishing trips and hiking trips and ball games. Sipping the coffee he couldn't rememeber ordering, he told her about raising a boy to be a man when he wasn't sure himself what it *meant* to be a man.

He told her briefly about a woman who hadn't been able to accept the presence of his brother in her life, and of Jason's only recently discovered feelings about that. He told her about the wrenching loneliness of Jason's college years and the final pang of seeing his brother a man grown and living apart from him.

And he told her of the guilt he felt now. Jason would have stayed in Chicago if he'd asked, not gone at all...

"You couldn't have known."

"I put him on that plane!"

"You couldn't have known, darling."

"He knew I needed to talk—and wouldn't. He

knew. He would have stayed if I'd asked. But I turned away from him. I couldn't talk to him. He saw me too clearly, and I couldn't bear that, so I put him on that plane."

"You needed to talk?"

Trevor nodded. He looked at her, forced a wry smile. "I was trying to come to terms with . . . how I felt about you."

Taylor didn't ask the question nine out of ten women would have asked. Not "How did you feel?" but a simple, "And you couldn't talk about that to him. I'm sure he understood, Trevor."

"But I've never been able to talk to him!" Trevor said savagely. "Not about anything that mattered. I've never told him I love him. I haven't even hugged him since he was a kid. God, I've made so many mistakes!"

"Jason's a fine man, isn't he?"

"Yes," Trevor said in a softer voice. "Yes, he is."

"Then your mistakes didn't hurt him. Trevor, you're human. You were a boy forced to be a man too soon, forced to shoulder his life as well as your own. But you did it. You raised your brother to be a fine man."

"I'm . . . proud of him," Trevor said, his voice almost inaudible. "And I've never told him that."

"You will."

"Unless it's . . . too late."

"It won't be."

He accepted that because he had to, needed to. And his own words set up an echo in his mind. *Too late . . . too late . . . too late . . .* He looked at her, saw her clearly, and realized that it wasn't too late for one thing, at least. He heard his own voice emerge, queerly conversational but strained.

"I love you, you know."

Taylor smiled slowly, eyes glowing. "I'm glad. I love you, too," she said simply.

Trevor barely heard the pilot announcing their descent into Casper; all his attention was focused on that beloved, fascinating face. "I couldn't tell you before. I was . . . afraid. I thought I needed time to . . . learn. Time to find out if I could give you what you needed."

"You have," she said, soft. "All I needed was your love, Trevor."

He realized then what he'd done. "All that about raising Jason," he said slowly. "I've never told anyone that before. I . . . needed to. But I never did. I was always afraid to . . . let it out."

"And now?"

With a sudden feeling of release, a feeling of burdens lifted, Trevor realized that the ghostly wall in his mind was gone. The fear and anxiety over Jason had driven him to talk, and he had instinctively reached out to the woman he loved. He looked at her wonderingly.

Taylor, gazing into that strong face that hid his vulnerability so well, felt the breath catch in her throat. He was looking at her, finally, as if he were finding what he wanted, needed, in her own face. As if, perhaps, he'd only just realized how much he needed. As if he were astonished and moved unbearably to see what he needed in her.

"And now I love you," he said huskily. "God, how I love you!" He leaned forward to kiss her tenderly.

The vivid blue eyes gazing softly into his were brighter than ever, and he realized only then that she was crying silently.

"Taylor . . ."

She laughed shakily, one hand lifting to touch her wet cheeks. "I'm crying because it matters," she marveled. "Finally because it matters. Oh, Trevor, I love you so much!"

They had shoved the world aside for those few precious moments, but now it intruded again as the plane touched down and taxied toward its particular gate. But the warmth of their love surrounded them both, cushioning against the chill of Jason's disappearance. Wrapped in that love, they automatically gathered their things and left the plane, Trevor's hand instantly catching hers once the narrow aisle had been left behind them.

A blond young man waited restlessly for them just inside the building, his lean face troubled and anxious. He greeted Trevor with "No word yet," and responded politely to the introduction to Taylor.

"I've chartered a helicopter to take us up to the lodge," he told them as they worked their way through the crowd. "The search teams are based there, coordinated by the Rangers."

It wasn't until they were in the noisy helicopter and lifting high in the chill air above Casper that a sudden thought occurred to Trevor. Using the headphones that made conversation possible, he asked Owen, "Did Jason leave any of his clothes at the lodge?"

"I think so," Owen called back. "Why d'you ask?"

Trevor looked at his love, and she responded with a decided nod. "The lady's psychic," he explained to Jason's friend. "Maybe she can find a trail for us."

Owen turned in his seat to favor Taylor with a long, interested look, then nodded. "I sure as hell hope so." He gestured worriedly at the sun sinking rapidly in the west. "We'll have at best a couple of hours of daylight left. The teams can search at night, but it's black as pitch up there. The Rangers'll probably want us to wait at the lodge after dark."

"If we haven't found Jason by dark, they'll want in vain," Trevor said calmly. He looked down at Taylor again. "Can you ride?" he asked quietly.

She nodded. "And I've ridden on mountain trails before."

He squeezed her hand. "I've been up here a couple of times with Jason," he told both her and Owen. "I know the area almost as well as he does."

Owen nodded, then hesitated before saying casually, "There's a doctor staying at the lodge."

Trevor only nodded in response, but his throat tightened. Almost instantly, he felt the warmth of the "security blanket" creeping over him. His own inner anguish had blocked that feeling until he had reached out to Taylor on the plane. Now he felt it wrapping him gently in strength and warmth, and he smiled down at Taylor, lifting her hand briefly to his lips.

"He'll be all right," she said firmly.

"Yes." He'd be all right. *He had to be all right.*

The helicopter touched down in a clearing near a rambling log building nestled in a high valley. A temperature quite a few degrees colder than they'd left in

Casper greeted them as they climbed out of the machine and hurried toward the lodge together.

Inside, they found a comfortable "hunters'" lodge, the pine-paneled walls hung with hunting and fishing trophies, the people milling about in the large lobby-den mostly men. All were dressed for warmth and preparing lanterns and strong flashlights, and all wore grim faces.

A swift question from Trevor caused them to drop their bags by the casual desk and turn quickly toward a tall man, his heavy jacket nearly hiding the uniform beneath. Trevor introduced himself and his two companions, discovering that Owen knew the man in charge of the rescue teams.

The Ranger, whose name was Pat Carmichael, favored the two strangers with a fleeting but keen once-over from tired brown eyes. "There isn't much I can tell you." He was speaking directly to Trevor. "We know he headed north, and we've combed all the lower trails. It'll take time to cover the higher ground, and that's something we may be short of if the weather prediction's accurate—and I think it will be. I've lived in these mountains too long not to know a storm's coming. If snow catches the searchers up on the high trails . . ."

He didn't have to finish the statement; Trevor knew full well that the search would have to be called off in bad weather. "If we can borrow some gear and horses," he said evenly, "you'll have three more for the search."

"Those mountain trails are tricky—"

"We'll manage."

The tired brown eyes measured him thoughtfully, then glanced down at Taylor. "How about the lady? No offense, ma'am."

"None taken," she said promptly. "I can manage, too, Mr. Carmichael. In fact, I may be able to shorten the search. If Jason left some clothes here, that is."

"How's that, ma'am?" he asked mildly.

She met his inquiring eyes squarely. "I'm psychic," she said bluntly. "I may be able to point us in the right direction."

The Ranger seemed to weigh her small, determined self, then nodded slightly. "Never believed in that myself," he said, still mild. "But I've seen stranger things in these mountains. And I'd be a fool to turn down any help offered—if Mr. King here was to *let* me turn it down, which I doubt. You're welcome, ma'am."

Taylor nodded and turned to Trevor. "I'll get his room key and check on the clothes."

He watched her hurry away, the warmth of her presence still with him; he realized then that he'd never lose it as long as he had her. With the Ranger's earlier bleak words ringing in his mind, he badly needed that warmth.

"Think she can find him?" Carmichael asked quietly.

Trevor met the other man's intent gaze. "I think she can find him," he responded, just as quiet.

The Ranger nodded, accepting. "You'll all need heavier coats than those you have," he said. "Hats and gloves, too. This way."

Taylor came back downstairs just in time to shrug

herself into the heavier coat Carmichael had found for her. It was a bit large but much warmer than her own quilted jacket. But she refused the proffered gloves. In her hand was a flannel shirt Trevor recognized as Jason's, and her eyes were more vivid than he'd ever seen them.

Carmichael protested her refusal of the gloves. "Ma'am, the temperature's dropping like a brick out there, your hands'll be frozen inside an hour!"

She shook her head firmly. "I have to be able to hold this—without gloves. I'll be fine."

Trevor took the gloves and silently put them in his pocket, as worried as the Ranger was about her hands but knowing better than to protest.

Sighing in defeat, Carmichael said only, "I suppose you know what you're doing, ma'am." He led the group outside, where a dozen horses waited, efficiently splitting the searchers into three groups and assigning the ground to be covered as well as a Ranger to each group. As Trevor had expected, Carmichael assigned himself to the three most concerned with Jason's well-being.

It would be a clear night boasting a full moon, a fact the Ranger wryly gave thanks for as he led the way from the lodge and up a gradually steepening trail. The horses were mountain-bred, carrying their riders easily and finding footholds where a goat would have balked.

The temperature dropped steadily.

Carmichael rode in the lead, with Taylor behind him. Then Trevor, with Owen bringing up the rear. It was still light enough to see without lanterns or flashlights, and they made good time for the first hour. Conversation was brief, dealing only with necessities. The Ranger kept in touch with the other search parties with a walkie-talkie, the negative reports drawing curt responses from him.

Taylor said almost nothing at all, but Trevor could glimpse from time to time her fingers moving over the shirt she held firmly. She rode easily, her slender body swaying to her horse's movements. She made no objection to the Ranger's choice of direction until they were slightly more than an hour from the lodge. Then, at a fork in the path they followed, she spoke up.

"Not that way."

Carmichael turned in the saddle as he halted his horse, looking at her searchingly through the gathering twilight. "That trail's no more than a rabbit lane, ma'am," he said, indicating the path he'd been on the point of ignoring. "It peters out after a hundred yards or so, and the rest is straight up. A man on foot—"

Fingering the shirt she held, Taylor pointed firmly with the hand grasping the reins. "That's the way he went."

"He wasn't wearing that shirt—" the Ranger objected, but was cut off fiercely.

"Not the shirt! *Him!* He went that way."

After a single glance at Trevor's face, Carmichael turned his horse toward the "rabbit lane." Clearly, though doubting the lady's judgment, he was unwilling to draw Trevor's defensive fire.

The trail narrowed as they moved along it, disappearing for good at the Ranger's estimate of a hundred yards. They had to pick their way cautiously, working around boulders and naked granite cliffs. The moon rose to provide some light, but flashlights were used more and more often to point ahead and search out obstacles. Taylor ordered a change in direction twice more, both times too definitely to invite argument.

And it was getting colder by the minute.

Three hours into the search, Taylor suddenly stopped her horse, her head moving in a horizon-sweeping gesture. "He's near," she said, the words misting in front of her face. "Close. Trevor—"

She didn't have to finish. *"Jason!"* he called out ringingly.

Echoes, then silence met their straining ears.

Taylor wasn't discouraged. She changed direction again, leading the way this time. After another hundred yards or so, she halted and glanced back at Trevor. Again, he shouted his brother's name.

Trevor strained to hear, all his concentration focused to catch the slightest sound. Was that—? Had he heard—?

She urged her horse forward, angling down a rocky slope with a sudden reckless haste.

"Be careful!" both Trevor and the Ranger shouted, urging their own horses to follow. They were only a few yards behind her when Taylor abruptly halted her horse and slid quickly from the saddle. And all three men reached her just as Taylor was lying flat on the crumbling edge of a ravine and peering down into the darkness.

"A flashlight!" she ordered breathlessly.

Carmichael halted Trevor as he started to cross the scant feet to the ravine's edge. "On your belly," he ordered tersely, handing the flashlight over. "And slowly; that edge could give way at any minute."

The edge . . .

Fear for her as well as Jason blocking his throat, Trevor lay flat and moved cautiously to her side. He flicked the flashlight on and pointed it over the edge, sweeping slowly along the bottom a good twenty feet below them. And the beam caught a red hunter's vest—necessary for a hiker wherever hunting was allowed—and eyes squinting out of a pale face. Taylor had been unerring; he was directly below them.

"Hey!" Jason called up to them in a faint voice.

Trevor had to swallow before he could respond. And relief made his response furious. "Jason, what the hell are you doing down there?"

"Mostly just lyin' here," Jason answered, rueful in spite of the exhausted voice. "Brother, you picked a dandy time to visit."

"Are you hurt?" Trevor called down, ignoring the humor although it made him feel better about Jason's condition.

"A few bruises and one slightly broken leg." Jason's voice faded toward the end of the sentence, then strengthened again. "I'm also a little cold and a lot thirsty—my canteen's empty, dammit."

"Hang on. I'll be down there in a minute," Trevor said, pulling Taylor with him as he eased back from the edge.

But in the end, it was Taylor who went down first. While Carmichael summoned the other searchers

and got the rope from his saddle, she was busy un-
fastening the backpack containing the first-aid kit from
her own saddle.

"I'm a doctor's daughter, Trevor, and I've worked
with him; I know as much as any paramedic. Besides,
I'm the lightest, and we don't know how much that
edge'll stand. Let me go down first."

Trevor argued, but the Ranger agreed with her once
he heard her reasoning, and even Trevor was forced
to give in when she briskly claimed experience in
belaying down more than one mountainside at the end
of a rope. So Taylor tucked two blankets and a thermos
of hot coffee into her pack, and the men very cautiously lowered her over the edge.

She obviously knew what she was doing, making
the descent quickly but safely.

A scant five minutes later, Trevor joined her in the
narrow, rock-strewn bottom of the ravine, untying the
rope and hurrying to kneel by his brother. He'd brought
two battery-powered lanterns with him, and with both
alight there was plenty of brightness.

Already Taylor had used her empty pack and Jason's
shirt to pillow his head, and he was half propped up
and sipping hot coffee gratefully, a blanket covering
all but the leg she was carefully and gently examining.

"Brat!" Trevor said roughly, gripping his brother's
shoulder.

Jason's face was pale with exhaustion, pain, and
shock, but the gray eyes gleamed with indomitable
spirit. "I know. And *such* a way to meet Taylor. Here
I was out of chocolate bars and water, counting stars
and hoping for rescue, and an angel lands beside me

with blankets and coffee." Jason reached a shaky hand up to grasp his brother's. For the first time, his voice faltered. "I'm so glad you found me."

"Me, too," Trevor said huskily, feeling the warmth of tears on his cold cheeks. "You rotten kid, how're you going to dance at my wedding with a broken leg?"

"I'll dance if it kills me!"

Taylor looked up just then, her eyes traveling from one brother to the other. "No broken ribs," she told them cheerfully. "Just bruises and a broken leg. Jason, are you *sure* there was no blurred vision or dizziness after you fell?"

He nodded. "None. I landed on the damned leg and then rolled. So, no concussion?"

"I don't think so. And no compound fracture; it's a clean break. It needs to be set and splinted before you're moved." She looked at him seriously. "I've set bones before, but it's going to hurt like hell. I think we'd better wait for the doctor; he could give you something for pain. He was in one of the other search parties, wasn't he, Trevor?"

Trevor nodded. "And Carmichael's called him; he should be here in about an hour."

Jason laughed unsteadily. "I can wait. This is heaven after the last two days. Trust me to decide to go for a last hike the morning I'm supposed to leave, and then find myself rolling headlong into some godforsaken gully!"

Chapter Nine

THE WAIT WAS slightly more than an hour. Warmed by the coffee and blankets, Jason was as comfortable as he could be. He insisted on hearing how they'd found him, and once he'd heard the whole story, he promised them both that he intended to shake Luke's hand. Then he pulled Taylor's head down and kissed her quite firmly, ignoring the stern rebuke from his brother.

"If you don't want her, I do," he said definitely.

Trevor gave him a mock frown. "I do want her." He looked at Taylor, adding silently, *God, do I want her!* And she smiled softly at him, clearly reading his thought without the need for telepathy.

Jason claimed their attention then by very seriously

thanking Trevor for drilling the basics of hiking into him years before. "I left about dawn and was just planning a few hours up here. But you were always so rabid on the idea of being prepared that I automatically stuck a couple of sandwiches and a handful of chocolate bars into the backpack." He gestured to the somewhat frayed canvas pack lying nearby with a canteen. "And I made sure I had plenty of water. It didn't really start getting cold until a few hours ago; last night was pretty mild."

"So you've been just fine," Trevor said ironically.

His brother grinned. "Well, it could have been worse."

Trevor poured more coffee for him, then handed Taylor her gloves, feeling the increasing chill in the air. Jason was, as he'd said, in much better shape than he might have been. No apparent concussion or broken ribs, and he was dressed warmly enough—although if he'd had to spend *this* night with no added protection against the steadily dropping temperatures . . . What Trevor was most worried about now was getting his brother out of this ravine and down the mountain.

Against all predictions, it seemed that the storm was approaching more quickly than expected. The moon was gone, and they could hear the wind rising in the trees high above them. And after Trevor followed the path of a single large snowflake as it drifted idly into their lamplight, his eyes rose to meet Taylor's. Her face was calm, but he could read the worried frown in her steady gaze.

Just then, there was a shout from above, and they looked up, barely able to make out a bulky form being lowered over the ravine's edge.

"The doctor," Taylor said instantly.

And so it proved to be. Introducing himself cheer-fully—"Just call me Doc`and we'll get along fine"—he knelt beside Jason and began unpacking an emer-gency medical kit far more extensive than the average first-aid box. He was deft and gentle, examining Jason quickly and asking a few questions almost identical to those Taylor had asked. He concurred in her belief that there was no concussion and instantly requested her help when her background as a doctor's daughter was disclosed.

The shot he gave Jason might not have eliminated all pain, but it made the bone-setting at least bearable. The leg was splinted firmly as a collapsible basket stretcher was lowered to them, and Jason was carefully transferred, wrapped as warmly as possible, and strapped in.

After a shouted conference with the men at the lip of the ravine, a complicated arrangement of ropes was lowered to them. A sturdy tree branch hanging out over the gully bore the weight of Jason's stretcher, while allowing him to be lifted more or less vertically. Trevor went up with him on his own rope, one hand firmly holding the basket to keep it steady.

The Rangers and their rescue teams, experienced in a variety of mountain mishaps, effected this part of the rescue quickly and safely. With Jason and Trevor out of the ravine, ropes were lowered for Taylor and the doctor, and both were safely brought up.

As for the trip down the mountain, that would live long in Trevor's nightmares. The storm burst upon them when they'd gone only a few hundred yards, pelting them with a mixture of sleet and snow and freezing them with an icy wind. Half a dozen of the men had volunteered to help carry Jason, the rest sent back to the lodge with the horses. In spite of Trevor's anxious request for Taylor to leave with the mounted men, she remained with them for the most hazardous beginning of the descent, leading her horse ahead of the rest to find the easiest path.

But once the worst was behind and they were on the main trail back to the lodge, she mounted her horse and headed back after asking the doctor what exactly he wanted to have waiting for them at the lodge. Trevor kissed her briefly before helping her to mount, offering no protest at her decision to hurry ahead. He'd seen enough to know she was an expert horsewoman, and the thought that his love could become lost was one to be dismissed the instant it occurred.

Not his Taylor.

And she didn't, of course. As the warmth of the lodge finally closed around rescuers and rescued, it became obvious that Taylor had used her hour's lead to the fullest extent. Her help had been gratefully accepted by the lodgekeeper's wife in preparing hot coffee and soup, and Jason's room awaited him with a cheerful fire in the hearth and everything the doctor required by the bed. Jason was carried to his room and left with only her and the doctor in attendance, since there was no question of trying to transport the injured man any distance in the worsening storm.

The Rangers and their teams, most of whom had been searching without rest for more than twenty-four hours, paused only to gulp coffee and soup before heading for needed rest. They brushed off Trevor's heartfelt thanks as unnecessary, but all gripped his hand firmly before seeking their beds. Owen, too, was thanked for his help, and went off to get a room for himself and take a hot shower.

Outside the lodge, the storm howled viciously.

Trevor ignored the soup but drank hot coffee as he waited to hear the news of Jason. He was worried, concerned that his brother might need more care than the lodge could provide, but he'd formed a good opinion of the doctor. He spent the time of waiting in requesting the last available room for himself and Taylor, unable to suppress a rueful comparison of this night to last night. Their bags were carried up, and he found himself alone in the lobby-den.

The doctor came down just before midnight, snaring a cup of coffee before sinking down beside Trevor on one of the wide couches near the fireplace. "Constitution of an ox," he said briefly after a sip.

Trevor felt relief sweeping over him. "He'll be all right?"

"I doubt he'll even have a cold after spending a night up there. He was warm enough, and didn't have to go too long without food and water. I'd feel better if I could X-ray that leg, but it's a very clean break and he had the sense not to try to move it. He's sleeping now, and I expect him to sleep all night. I'll check on him during the night, but no one else needs to."

"Thank you—"

"I'll send you the bill." The doctor grinned at him,

his weathered face cheerful. "For now, I've sent your lady off to have a hot shower, after which she's under orders to get something hot inside her. You do the same. This storm won't be letting up anytime soon, but your brother'll be fine up here until we can get him to Casper."

Trevor wasn't surprised when the older man brushed off a second attempt to thank him. Left alone again, he stared into the fire for a while, a little numb from the emotional battering of the day. Then he made a quiet request of the lodgekeeper's wife after apologizing for all the trouble. She responded by cheerfully disclaiming any trouble, complimenting him on "your lady," and assuring him she'd send a tray up to their room.

He stopped by Jason's room, going in to assure himself that his brother was indeed all right. Standing by the bed and gazing down at that sleeping face that was younger but very like his own, he remembered other night vigils, other injuries and childhood illnesses. Absently, he leaned over to tuck in a stray corner of the bright quilt, hearing his own husky voice in the peaceful quiet of the room.

"You've grown into a fine man, Jase. Maybe one day I'll be able to tell you how proud I am of you."

Green eyes opened to look up into his own, drowsy and warm with love. "You just did," Jason murmured. His hand fumbled to grip his brother's tightly. "But you've told me before . . . in different ways." The grip loosened as weariness and the painkillers pulled him back toward sleep, his last words almost inaudible. ". . . love you . . ."

Very gently, Trevor slid the hand back under the warmth of the covers. "I love you, too, Jase," he whispered. He straightened slowly, then turned away from the lamplit bed.

Taylor stood in the doorway watching silently, vivid eyes very bright and full. She was wearing a floor-length terry robe, having obviously just come from her shower. When he reached the door, she slid her arms around his waist in a fierce hug that he welcomed and returned, then spoke softly as they stepped out into the hall and pulled the door shut behind them.

"The doctor ordered hot showers; it's your turn."

He kept one arm around her as they moved down the hall. "And hot food; Mrs. Clay's sending up some of her—and your—soup."

She smiled up at him as they entered their room. It was a large and comfortable bed-sitting room with a huge four-poster bed, its covers drawn back welcomingly, near a curtained window, and a couch and small table set up to flank a fireplace a few feet from the door. The bathroom opened off one side, and the double closet off the other.

"If you feel like I did," she said, "you're probably cold to the bone. Go take your shower."

He did, standing under the hot water until his tingling skin protested. Then he dried off and pulled on his own terry robe. His fingers sufficed to comb his damp hair. When he stepped out into the room, he found Taylor sitting at the small table with a tray in front of her, sipping coffee as she stared into the flickering fire.

Trevor sat down across from her and firmly pushed

a bowl of soup toward her. "Eat."

"I will if you will."

Smiling, he took the second bowl, and they both began eating. Nothing more was said until the soup was finished: then Trevor spoke first. "You must be exhausted."

"Oddly enough, no." Her smile was a little crooked. "How about you?"

"No. Just—relieved."

"I know. I'm so glad Jason'll be all right."

"We should call your parents," he said idly.

"I already did, while you were in the shower. Daddy knew Jason was all right, though."

Trevor chuckled softly. "I keep forgetting."

"Does it still bother you? My being psychic?"

Instantly, he rose from the table and went around to gently pull her to her feet, his arms closing round her. "We wouldn't have found Jason without you," he said soberly. "How could it bother me?"

"It did once," she reminded him, her voice diffident.

"Only because I didn't think I could share enough of myself with you. But now I want to share everything with you. I want you to share everything with me. I love you, Taylor. And I don't need any more time to be sure of that."

Her arms slipped up around his neck, and a smile slowly grew in her brilliant eyes. "If I were a scrupulous woman," she murmured, "I'd say something about catching you with your guard down. After a day like we've had, I've no right to take you at your word."

"But you aren't a scrupulous woman?"

"Not where you're concerned."

Trevor drew her even closer, feeling the warmth of her slender body against his. "Take me at my word, Taylor," he urged softly, huskily. "Today may have speeded things up, but I've known for a long time that we belonged together. I've realized that time isn't a commodity we can count on; I don't want to waste another moment of our time together."

She smiled, achingly sweet and inviting. "There's no candlelight," she whispered. "No French perfume. No black lace and garters. There's just a blizzard outside, and inside the scent of soap and the crackle of a fire."

He reached back to turn off the light switch, leaving the room lit only by that fire. "Much as I adore your parents, I think we can get along without their advice—tonight. We don't need seductive props, sweetheart." The endearment felt warm in his heart, right in his mouth.

He lifted her easily in his arms, carrying her slight weight across the room to the wide bed and then setting her gently back on her feet. His hands lifted to cradle her face, bending his head until the warm silk of her lips touched his. He felt her response growing, strengthening, even as his own desire, never absent, began to build achingly.

Like the first time he'd kissed her, Trevor felt himself opening to receive a warm, soul-deep radiance. It spread throughout his body, a bright and glowing fire, and this time he felt no panicked urge to draw away from that. Instead, he gloried in it, recognizing the truth of two minds and two spirits striving to become one.

He felt terry cloth beneath his fingers as he pushed the robe off her shoulders, then his own robe sliding to the floor. Lifting his head, he gazed down at the slender body painted by the firelight's golden touch, the breath catching in his throat, his heart pounding against his ribs. He lifted her again and lowered her to the bed, easing his own weight beside her.

"You're so beautiful," he whispered, only dimly hearing the ragged break in his own voice. "Taylor..."

The touch of her hands on his shoulders was silken fire, the murmur of his name in her throat a siren song of winging need. Blue eyes looked at him with trust and desire. If the wind howled outside the curtained window, it was a distant and unimportant thing, dimmed in the spiraling wildness of thudding hearts and uneven breaths. He was lost somewhere in a world containing only satin flesh beneath his hands and lips, and the fiery, radiant heat of desperate longing.

"Trevor..."

Lost, and he didn't care. Whispering he knew not what, except her name, always her name, he drew the soft curves and hollows of her body on his soul. His hands trembled with the strength of what he felt as they shaped and stroked, feeding his hunger. He was starving for her, the ache inside him growing until it was an unbearable hollowness.

His lips pressed hot, tender kisses over her face, her throat; endearments jerked from his own throat, from deep in his chest. The vibrant need for her breasts drew his mouth, intensified the hunger that couldn't be satisfied by mere touch or taste.

Trembling bodies moved restlessly, seeking satisfaction. Trevor could feel the feverish heat of her body beneath his hands and lips, even as his own body seemed to him an inferno. They were both burning out of control.

Brilliant blue eyes darkened with need gazed into his own, a soft plea reaching his ears. Desperate as his own need was, he moved sensitively, gentling her seeking body to accept him as a part of herself. And there was no awkwardness, only a smooth and tender joining, a possession that was hers and his and richly complete.

In the first instant's hesitation and savoring, in the momentary stillness, Trevor felt the soft, caressing touch of her mind as all senses opened to her. With quicksilver warmth and joy, her thoughts became his in a communication deeper than any he could have imagined. The stark aloneness of one mind became the unshadowed sharing of two, a breathless, joyous communion and recognition of spirit.

The fulfillment of mental bonding was a blinding glow, surrounding and feeding the physical passion, driving it higher and higher, driving them toward a consummation of the flesh. Need soared, their bodies matching in a yearning rhythm until they could go no higher, no further, until there was only a soul-jarring ecstasy and only each other to cling to...

In the quiet of the room there was no sound but the soft crackle of the fire. Trevor held her close to his side, still dazed, stunned, still not quite certain he wouldn't wake in the morning alone both physically and mentally. But he could feel the softest of touches in his mind, not an intrusion but simply an open door, an easy link with the mind of his love.

An open door.

Instinctively, tentatively, he sent a jumbled message through that door, a tangled, passionate declaration. And it was returned instantly to him in full, soft with love and an aching sweetness. He felt alight from within, warm as he'd never been before, and knew a sudden, heartfelt pity for the sense-blind majority of mankind.

To not know this—!

"I love you," he murmured, because there was still the inescapable human need to voice aloud what the heart knew so well.

She lifted her head to smile at him, the wonderful eyes brilliant. "I love you, darling. So very much."

He returned the smile as his hand lifted to stroke the vibrant silk of her hair. "You should have given me a good, swift kick days ago," he scolded gently. "God—I've been fighting *this?*"

Taylor rested her chin atop the hand lying on his chest, her own smile turning rueful. "I did try," she reminded him.

After a moment's thought, Trevor nodded slowly. "Yes. But I had to try as well, didn't I?"

"You had to meet me halfway. It was always your choice, darling. I knew we belonged together, and the emotional certainty was there by the end of that first day. But *you* had to be that certain."

"And on the plane," he realized aloud, "I ... needed you."

"You were afraid for Jason," she said tenderly. "So afraid. You needed to share him—and you—with someone else. You had to talk about the two of you. You had to keep him alive in your mind, to fight the fear of losing him."

"And you?" He looked at her gravely. "You cried on the plane—because it mattered."

"You let me in," she said simply. "You trusted me with all the love and pain of your life. And you looked at me as if—as if everything you needed was me. With you beside me now, I think I'll always be able to cry when it matters."

He drew her head forward to kiss her gently. "This ... mental link between us. Were you expecting that?"

She laughed. "Darling, in case you haven't realized it yet, you have powerful psychic abilities of your own!"

"I do?"

Taylor laughed again at his blankness. "You certainly do. I felt a touch of it in you that first day, but when you finally opened up ... It's been locked inside you all these years, just waiting for an outlet. Haven't you felt moments of perception, flashes of intuitive certainty that you doubted at the time but that turned out to be accurate?"

Thinking about it clearly, Trevor realized that he had. Moments when he'd been certain how a jury would vote, moments when he had focused on some seemingly unimportant detail in a client's defense, only to find the entire case unlocked. "Good Lord," he said faintly. "Will I—will I be aware of it when it happens now?"

"Not at first," she said. "You'll automatically consider it just a part of your thought processes. I think you'll get stronger, though, now that you can let it out."

"I wonder if Jason—"

"Of course," she said casually, then giggled at his startled blink. "Trevor, because you had to be strong for Jason all those years, you gave him the chance to be vulnerable; there are no shields in his mind the way yours was shielded. And there's a bond between you that's more than blood. I think he reached out to you without even realizing what he was doing; otherwise, Daddy would never have picked up that he was in trouble. *You* were still guarding yourself, and I can never pick up a thought without physical touch of a person or object."

"I thought Luke was the precognitive one," was all Trevor could say.

"He is. But he's telepathic in a peculiar way. With all his children, and with Mother, it's an automatic, unthinking thing. With others, he's erratic. Jason reached out, and Daddy just happened to be the only one listening."

The central point of the conversation had Trevor a bit dazed. "So you're telling me that both myself and Jason are psychic?"

With a solemn face and dancing eyes, Taylor nodded. "You're the strongest, though. Jason could probably communicate pretty well with another psychic, one who knew how to reach. But you won't even need that, given time."

It was then that Trevor remembered two vaguely troubling encounters with her sisters, "Dory—and Jess. They both knew."

"Did they?" Taylor asked, interested.

He nodded slowly. "Dory asked me about my— my closed door." He looked at Taylor, unsurprised to see her comprehension.

"We use that so she'll understand better and learn to shield her own mind."

"I guessed that. But when she asked me about my own closed door, I just thought..."

"That since you weren't psychic, she'd confused no ability with the ability to *hide* ability?"

"Something like that. When I explained to her that I couldn't hear things the way she could, she... laughed. Then she smiled at me and said, 'You don't know.' I couldn't figure out what she meant. But now ... She knew."

Taylor nodded. "Dory's going to be strong. And Jess?"

"When I denied being psychic, she didn't seem to believe me."

"Be sure to tell her she was right," Taylor advised calmly. "Jess has always felt a little left out—being less psychic, I mean."

"You knew that?"

"Of course. But it didn't do any good for any of us to reassure her. It was you encouraging her with the music that helped, darling."

Trevor shook his head a little helplessly. "I can't get over it. I'm psychic. I'm psychic?"

"You certainly are."

A little surprised at his bemused acceptance of this,

Trevor suddenly found himself laughing.

"What's so funny?" she asked, smiling, knowing.

"Me," he said ruefully. "I was so worried about sharing my mind with you. But now, it's like—like I've been only half alive and never knew it."

"So was I," she confided quietly. "Building shields . . . locks yourself in as well as others out. There's a part of me no one's touched but you. Oh, Trevor, I never knew it could feel this way!"

"I'm very glad I found you crying in that park, love."

She snuggled closer contentedly, her head resting on his shoulder. Then, only a quick flash of mental laughter alerting him, her ridiculous sense of humor reared its head.

"It *would* have been nice if you'd chased me to Australia," she mourned.

"I wouldn't have done that in any case, " he said stoutly.

"No?"

"No. I would never have let you start the trip."

A note of suspicion crept into her voice. "You wouldn't have?"

"Absolutely not."

"You'd have flung me over your saddle and galloped off with me?" Pleasure was growing in her voice.

"Something like that."

"You'd have put your foot down and *ordered* me not to go?"

"Closer."

"You'd have grabbed me and shaken me and *com-*

manded me not to go?" she asked delightedly.

Trevor bit back a laugh. "Definitely. I'd have stuck you in a castle, raised the drawbridge, and put alligators in the moat."

"Because—?"

"Because, you adorable little witch, I can't live without you."

Taylor sighed happily. "Prince Charming. At last."

He hugged her, then said suddenly, "I forgot."

"What did you forget?"

"To propose," he said wryly. "Of course, I realize that in the eyes of your family, the ceremony's only a formality."

"But a proposal's obligatory," she said in a firm tone.

"In that case, will you marry me, love?"

"I'll have to think about it."

"Witch."

She giggled. "This is so sudden! We haven't even known each other a *month*, for heaven's sake! I hardly know you, sir!"

Trevor made a rude noise.

She giggled again. "I couldn't resist."

"Neither can I. *Answer* me, for godsake! My heart and all my worldly possessions are at your feet! My castle beckons to you!"

"I never could resist castles."

"Is that a yes?"

"An unqualified yes, darling."

"I'm not Prince Charming, you know," he felt honor-bound to point out.

"No, but you're *mine*," she responded serenely.

"And you're mine." There was a world of contentment in his voice.

"D'you think we should elope?" she asked, thoughtful.

"Are you kidding? I want a double-ring ceremony with all the flourishes, my love."

"Yes, but, Trevor—my family."

"They can come," he conceded magnanimously.

"I'm serious! You *know* my family. It'll be the most absurd wedding in history."

"I know." He chuckled softly. "I wouldn't miss it for the world."

She laughed as well. "If you don't mind, I don't."

"Then all that remains is to set the date."

"June?"

"That's too far away," he protested.

"We're almost into May now, darling, and if you want a big wedding..."

He sighed. "June it is, then. Where would you like to go on our honeymoon?" He was vaguely aware that sleep was tugging at him, and her own voice held a touch of drowsiness when she answered.

"Anywhere, darling. As long as we're together."

"We will be, love. We will be."

Chapter Ten

TAYLOR PULLED THE young Siamese cat off the dining room table and put him firmly on the floor. "Pyewacket, you know better than that," she said absently. She barely heard the cat's disgusted "Hrrooo!" because she was busy deciding if she'd forgotten anything.

"Grandmother's china, best napkins, candles, wine..." She checked the wine in its terra-cotta cooler, then nodded, satisfied.

She went back into the kitchen, watching where she walked because Pye's favorite game was tripping his humans. The frustrated cat grumbled at her, but she gave him only a rueful smile. "You'd better hide when Trevor gets home," she advised. "You stole his best cuff link this morning, and he hasn't forgiven you for that." Pye's second-favorite game was stealing.

Taylor tasted from several bubbling dishes, added a few spices to one, then glanced at the clock on the wall. Good. She'd timed it perfectly. He'd be home any time now, and they had the whole weekend ahead...

She reached for the phone as it shrilled a summons, amused even before she got the receiver to her ear. "Hello, Mother."

"Darling, does he know yet?"

"Honestly, there are no secrets in a family of psychics!" Taylor rolled her eyes heavenward ruefully. "I haven't told him yet, and I don't *think* he knows."

"Tonight?"

"That's what I've planned. How's Amanda, Mother?"

"Flourishing," Sara replied vaguely. "She kept us up last night, but your father's spoken to her. Dory says she's going to have green eyes. So nice and sweet. Different, too."

"Well, say hello to her for us."

"I will, darling. Oh, Taylor—"

"Yes, Mother?"

"Twins. Your father's sure."

"I was pretty sure myself," Taylor murmured.

"So nice. Lots of babies," Sara said. "Our love to Trevor, darling."

Taylor was giggling when she hung up the phone. She was still working as her father's receptionist but had gone to another doctor for her tests; Luke didn't treat his own family except in emergencies. Still, there were no secrets in her family.

Leaning back against the counter, she thought back over the last months. Six months since the wedding, a week since her baby sister's birth. And only two weeks until Christmas. If Taylor hadn't been psychic, she would have considered it a good bet that her own babies would be born very near the first anniversary of her marriage; being psychic, she was positive. *On* the anniversary. June twentieth—a Friday.

Friday's child is loving and giving.

.Perfect.

In fact, everything was perfect. She and Trevor had found this old house and restored it gradually during the past months, with help from Jason and from her father. She smiled suddenly, wondering if her husband had noticed his brother's fascinated interest in Jamie. Of course he'd noticed; Trevor missed very little these days.

Jamie was still a very young woman, but Jason had clearly made up his own mind. He'd wait for her, Taylor thought. Jamie kept her own counsel, but Taylor knew her sister. And wouldn't they make a wonderful couple—Jason so lively and Jamie so serene. Complicated explaining the situation to outsiders. Her husband's brother was also her sister's husband?

Oh, well.

She looked through the kitchen window at the snow blanketing their large yard and listened. Moments later, the back door swung open, admitting Trevor and a blast of arctic cold. He shut the door hastily.

"Why," he demanded wryly, "do we live in Chicago?"

"Because we both grew up here." Happily, Taylor

went into his arms as soon as he shed his coat. She'd stopped wondering if each kiss would be as warmly dizzying as the last, content in the knowledge that it would.

How she loved this man!

The inner change in him had wrought an outward change as well. His gray eyes smiled now, gleaming with love and laughter. His lean, handsome face was relaxed and seemed years younger. He was quick to sense moods in those around him, quicker still to sensitively adapt himself to those moods.

Their love was a large part of that, of course, but the jolting truth of time's fragility had also changed him. Trevor had learned in a single fear-filled day never to take time for granted.

Though all barriers had crashed into rubble that day, it hadn't been easy for Trevor. His growing closeness with Jason had been a tentative, sometimes awkward thing, but immensely rewarding. And just as difficult had been his complete acceptance of his own psychic abilities; that still startled him, and probably would, she thought, for a while yet.

His wife had no complaints at all. With her, Trevor had opened up instantly and completely. The door that had opened that blustery night in Wyoming had never closed, he as comfortable with it as she was. And the love and laughter they'd shared since that night only confirmed and enhanced what both felt.

He was looking down at her now in faint surprise after glancing through to the dining room. "Candles— wine." His arms tightened around her. "What's the occasion, love?"

"I could say it was my birthday," she teased.

"That's in April," he said firmly. "April first, as a matter of fact. Apt, I've always thought."

"You were disappointed to find that out," she reminded him, turning away to check her preparations for dinner. "You were hoping I'd been born on Halloween—to fit in beautifully with your witch theme!"

As if in conditioned response, Trevor bent to pick up the cat nattering at his feet. "Well, slightly disappointed," he said sheepishly, allowing Pyewacket to climb onto his shoulder. "And you didn't answer my question."

"Didn't I?"

"You grow more like Sara every day!" he said severely.

Taylor giggled. "Sorry." Not that he seemed to mind. "Actually, I just thought I'd try seducing you again."

"You did that last night."

"I did not. I distinctly remember you joining me in the shower. I didn't do a single thing to provoke seduction."

"If standing there with only a bar of soap in one hand and a washcloth in the other isn't provoking, I don't know what is!"

"*I* was minding my own business."

He matched her virtuous tone. "And *I* was merely betraying a perfectly normal husbandly concern. I thought you might have drowned."

She started laughing. "Oh, put the cat down and make yourself useful!"

"Yes, ma'am."

* * *

They never ran out of things to say to each other, so it wasn't until dinner had been finished and the kitchen cleaned that Taylor got around to her reason for the special meal.

The stereo was loaded with soft music, a fire kindled in the large old stone hearth in the den. Pyewacket had curled up in his basket near the fireplace, sleepy after his own dinner. And his two humans were sharing the large couch only a few feet away from him.

Trevor was sitting on the end of the couch, Taylor turned so that she half lay across his lap. One of his hands stroked her long hair, as he often did, and the other rested lightly but possessively on her hip.

Deciding that the time was right, she spoke casually into the peaceful silence. "Darling?"

The gray eyes smiled tenderly down at her. "Yes, love?"

"I asked you a question once. You said I should ask you later."

Trevor, not gifted with Jason's total recall, was puzzled. "I don't remember the question, but ask away."

She absently parted the top buttons of his shirt, her fingers seeking the crisp hair beneath. "I asked if you wanted babies," she murmured. Her attention fixed on his chest, she only lifted her eyes back to his when the silence had stretched.

An arrested expression held the slate-gray eyes, and his face was very still. "Taylor . . .?" he breathed.

Her smile growing, Taylor nodded.

Trevor pulled her closer in a sudden fierce, gentle

hug. "I do want babies," he said huskily. "Our babies." Then, whether through the ever-present contact they shared or through his own strengthening abilities, Trevor understood the rest. A slightly unsteady hand lifted her chin, and he gazed at her, bemused. "Twins?"

"I'm pretty sure." She laughed softly. "The doctor doesn't know that yet, but Mother called and said Daddy was certain."

He hugged her again, held her for a long time. "I love you, witch," he murmured. "So much."

"I love you too, darling."

"I'm so glad I found you crying in that park." He laughed suddenly. "You never have told me what you were crying about that day."

Taylor smiled, remembering. She didn't cry about unimportant things any longer. In fact, not counting the time she'd deliberately made herself cry to tease Trevor, that day in the park had seen her last unimportant tears.

Unimportant! Those tears had changed her life.

"I was crying because somebody had stepped on a rose."

Trevor shook his head, rueful, tender. "Somebody stepped on a rose, and I ended up married to a psychic—*and* finding myself psychic."

"Life's funny, isn't it?" she observed solemnly.

"Love"—he laughed on a sigh, his eyes full of silver warmth, the arms holding her gentle and strong beyond belief—"you've taught me the truth of that. Life is funny. And so much more now than I ever thought it could be."

Taylor lifted her face for his kiss, a part of her

wishing she *had* been born on Halloween, just to make Trevor's life utterly perfect. But it was all right, really. She'd always be his witch. And an April witch had powers an October witch could never match.

Magic.

COMING NEXT MONTH

SECOND CHANCE AT LOVE

Be Sure to Read These New Releases!